THE BACHELOR'S
BABY DILEMMA

BY
SHERI WHITEFEATHER

MILLS &
BOON

Published in Great Britain 2015
by Mills & Boon, an imprint of Harlequin (UK) Limited,
Eton House, 18-24 Paradise Road, Richmond, Surrey, TW9 1SR

© 2015 Sheree-Henry Whitefeather

ISBN: 978-0-263-25121-0

23-0315

"Don't worry. You're going to be okay."

"And so are you. With your niece, I mean."

Tanner smiled. "We're always telling each other that everything will be all right."

"So it seems." Candy wanted to wrap her arms around him and indulge herself in a body-warming hug. But they'd yet to embrace, and this wasn't the time to start. She knew better than to risk it, especially when the mystery of his bedroom was just around the bend.

"I chose a magical horse for you to ride today," he said, drawing her into a new conversation.

"Magical?"

"A white horse. All she needs is a sparkly gold horn to look like a unicorn."

"Unicorns were my girlish obsession." She thought about the stress associated with her youth, the perfection that had been expected of her. "Sometimes I used to imagine disappearing into a world of make-believe and never coming back."

"Now's your chance. For a few hours, anyway."

"What's the mare's name?"

"Enchanted."

"That's beautiful, Tanner." It was as close to magic as a grown-up girl like Candy could get.

Family Renewal:
Sometimes all it takes is a second chance.

Sheri WhiteFeather is an award-winning, bestselling author. She writes a variety of romance novels for Mills & Boon and has become known for incorporating Native American elements into her stories. She has two grown children who are tribally enrolled members of the Muscogee Creek Nation. She lives in California and enjoys shopping in vintage stores and visiting art galleries and museums. Sheri loves to hear from her readers at www.sheriwhitefeather.com.

Chapter One

Candy McCall didn't want to sell her house. It was her dream home, her Southern California sanctuary, and she was going to miss it when she was gone.

Of course it hadn't sold yet. She hadn't even gotten any offers. That might change today, though. A potential buyer was on his way. And of all things, she'd discovered that it was someone from her past. Her very first boyfriend, in fact. A man named Tanner Quinn. She hadn't seen him since they were teenagers or kept track of his whereabouts, but they had a mutual friend who'd referred him to her.

She'd spoken to him briefly on the phone and learned that he owned a place called T.Q.'s Riding Academy and Stables. Oh, and that if he was interested in her house, it would be a cash sale.

She closed her eyes and said a quick prayer. A cash

sale was just what she needed to get out of this mess. She was in such a dire financial situation she couldn't even afford to use a Realtor.

But how strange was this going to be, showing her house to Tanner? She was actually nervous about seeing him.

Just as she opened her eyes, the doorbell rang.

She rushed to answer the summons, then gazed at the man on her porch. *Heaven almighty.* That six-foot-three frame. Those slate-gray eyes. He would be around her age, thirty-four or so now, and although he'd grown up and filled out, she would know him anywhere.

With his short black hair slicked away from his handsomely chiseled face, he made quite the dashing figure. He wore a classic ensemble of English riding gear. Clearly, he'd just come from work. Or a polo match. Or something where wicked boots were required.

Neither of them spoke. They just kept staring at each other, with awkward smiles, trying to get used to this hasty reunion.

He finally said, "Well, hello, Candy Sorensen."

"Hello, yourself. But for the record, I'm Candy McCall now," she reminded him.

"Oh, that's right. Your married name."

"Yes." She paused and uncomfortably added, "But as I mentioned on the phone, I'm divorced now." The dissolution of her marriage was a painful topic, but she couldn't very well behave as if she was still a doe-eyed wife. Changing the subject, she gestured to the doorway. "Do you want to come in?"

She stepped back to allow him entrance, and he crossed the threshold, looking like the horseman that he was. She wasn't surprised that he made his living in the equestrian industry. He'd always worked around horses, except that he'd been more of the cowboy type when he was younger.

Then again, she didn't doubt he would be just as comfortable in Wrangler jeans and a Stetson as he was in a button-down shirt and breeches, or that he still rode Western-style.

Trying to keep a professional air, she took a deep breath, preparing to treat him like the potential buyer he was. But he wasn't glancing around her living room or paying attention to the house he'd come to see.

Instead, he swept his gaze over her. "You sure as hell look good. But you always did."

"Yes, picture-perfect me." There went her professionalism. She made a doll-like motion, mocking herself. Candy was a long, lean, leggy brunette who'd spent her youth parading around in beauty pageants and hating every second of it.

He broke into a smile. "You still can't take a compliment after all this time? Some things never change."

She hoped he was wrong about that. She didn't want to think of herself as the same people-pleaser she'd been back then. She'd never had to please him, though. He'd accepted her for who she was. She'd always liked that about him.

He moved toward the fireplace, the mottled stones enhancing the color of his eyes. "Are you selling your house because of the divorce?"

"No." She kept her response vague, not wanting to get into the money issue. "It doesn't have anything to do with that."

"I've never been married." He frowned a little. "But I prefer being a bachelor."

Was he thinking about his parents' troubled marriage and how it had disintegrated after his infant sister had died? Or was his frown something altogether different?

She certainly remembered the devastation from the past. Candy had been there that morning, playing video games with Tanner, when his frantic mother had found the lifeless baby in her crib.

"How's your family?" she asked, needing to know about them, needing to hear that they were fine.

"Kade is a horse trainer, but he's on the road a lot, doing clinics and whatnot, so I don't see him all that much. But we call each other when we can."

The older brother. She'd only met him once, when he'd come home for the baby's funeral. Otherwise he'd been away at college, studying equine science. Apparently he was still away, in some form or another.

"We don't talk to our dad anymore," Tanner said. "Too much water under that bridge. Mom was always there, of course, with her nurturing ways. But then she died last year."

A stream of sadness swept over her. So much for everyone being fine. "I'm so sorry. She was such a nice lady. I always liked her."

"She liked you, too. She used to marvel at how much Meagan adored you."

Meagan was his other little sister, a spitfire of a child who'd needed mounds of attention. "Remember how she was always pestering me to curl her hair? And paint her nails? And put makeup on her?"

"Of course I remember. She wanted to be just like you. She was pissed at me after you and I broke up. She kept asking me when I was going to bring you back. But then Buffy became her idol, and she let me off the hook."

Candy feigned offense, especially since he was smiling once again. "I was replaced by a vampire slayer?"

"Afraid so. But Meagan was only eight. She didn't know any better. Now, if I'd dropped you like a hot potato for Buffy and her Scooby gang, it would have been another story."

She swatted his arm, and he laughed. But just as quickly, they both went serious again. He hadn't dropped her, not in the way he'd just suggested. Their breakup had been more of a moody drift. After the baby died and his parents started going through their messy divorce, Tanner began to retreat into himself, becoming more and more detached. Finally, it reached a point where he couldn't handle having a girlfriend anymore.

Candy, on the other hand, had longed to have another boyfriend, which, eventually, led to Vince, the handsome heartbreaker she'd married.

"After you and I broke up, my mom said that I was being a jerk," Tanner said.

Her pulse jumped. "What?"

"She didn't like how I ended it with you. She was critical of my behavior because of my dad. But I wasn't like him. I was just a kid, trying to cope with it all."

"I remember how difficult it was for you." She also recalled the big blasting hurt of being rejected by him, even if it hadn't been as callous as the way Vince had kicked her to the curb. Before the past got the better of her, she changed the subject. "Speaking of kids, you never said what Meagan does for a living. Does she work with horses, too?"

"No. She isn't a horsewoman. And she's not a kid

anymore, either," he added. "She's twenty-five now, and her situation is complicated."

She waited for him to expound, but he didn't. Whatever was going on with Meagan, he obviously didn't want to talk about it.

A moment later, he asked, "How's your family?"

She answered the question, loaded as it was. "My grandparents are gone, so it's just me and my mom now." She didn't have a dad. He'd died when she was three, and her mom rarely spoke of him, even when Candy prodded her for information.

"Did you ever become a model?" Tanner asked. "The way you were supposed to?"

She tugged unglamorously at the hem of her top. "Yes, I followed the career path Mom chose for me. But I wasn't as successful as she would've liked." She quit tugging and smoothed the fabric. "I'm a yoga instructor now. I teach doga, too. Yoga for dogs," she clarified.

"Really? Oh, that's cute. I'd like to see that sometime."

As if on cue, her faithful companion, a yellow Lab, moseyed in through the back door. Candy made the introduction. "That's Yogi. She's my best student."

"Hey, there," Tanner said, prompting the dog to come forward and greet him.

He knelt to pet her, running his fingers through her luxurious fur. Yogi all but melted from his touch, pressing closer to his hand. Candy considered correcting her, but the poor thing wasn't doing anything wrong. Besides, she knew the feeling, remembering how Tanner used to touch her, too.

Lightly, magically, but without taking it too far.

Good girl that she was, Candy had been saving herself for marriage—a choice that had backfired when she'd met Vince. She'd let her ex pressure her into being with him, long before there was even a hint of marriage.

So what did that say about the decision she'd made? That she should have just gone ahead and made Tanner her first?

As he righted his posture, bringing his big, broad body back to its full height, she warned herself not to think along those lines.

She steered the conversation back to business. "Do you want to walk around by yourself? Or do you want me to give you a tour?"

"I'd rather have you show me the place."

"Would it be all right if we start with the backyard?" Candy needed a big old gulp of fresh air. "Then I can show you the guesthouse and we can come back here and finish the tour."

"Sure. That's fine. We can start wherever you want."

She led the way, and they ventured outside, stood on the patio and studied her yard, where an English-style garden, rife with flowers, trees and vine-covered trellises, made for a colorful presentation.

She said, "I have a gardener who mows the lawn and rakes the leaves, but I tend to the rest of it myself. I love working in the flowerbeds."

"I don't know anything about flowers. But it looks like a nice garden." He stepped onto the lawn. "Eric told me that you hosted his wedding."

She fell into step beside him. Eric was the friend they had in common. But their association with him wasn't from their teenage days. It was much more recent. "Eric and Dana got married here. It was a beautiful ceremony."

"I haven't met Dana yet."

"She's amazing. She's my dearest friend. I'm their son's godmother. He's a toddler now. And so darned cute. Eric has an older daughter, too. She's in college, studying at UCLA."

"I remember her when she was younger."

"Really?" Surprised, she asked, "So just how long have you known Eric?" Clearly, much longer than she had.

"About eight or nine years, I think, but we lost touch after his first wife died. Then we ran into each a few weeks ago and started getting caught up again."

"I guess that explains why you and I haven't crossed paths before now." And why Tanner hadn't been at the wedding. "I've only known Eric since he and Dana got together."

"Mostly I hung out with him on the powwow circuit."

Candy nodded. Tanner was part Cheyenne, and Eric was half Cherokee. "Did you know his first wife?"

"Yes. He grieved something awful when she passed." Tanner stood beside a lemon tree, the bright yellow fruit in full bloom. Silent, he studied the branches, then turned to look at her. "I've been thinking about Ella a lot lately."

She inhaled the citrusy scent, trying to take comfort in it. Ella was his sister who'd died. "I'm sorry that her loss still affects you."

"You have no idea. The complication I mentioned earlier involves a baby. Meagan is pregnant."

Jarred by his words, she sucked in her breath. Candy had been pregnant once upon a time, but she'd miscarried, losing the child she'd so desperately wanted.

She quietly asked, "Is she having a difficult time

carrying the baby?" Was Meagan in danger of losing her little one?

"No. She seems to be doing okay in that regard. But she got into some trouble with the law and is serving time. She worked at an accounting firm and embezzled from some of their clients."

"Oh, my goodness." The spunky eight-year-old who used to follow Candy around like a rosy-cheeked puppy had morphed into a criminal? "When is her baby due?"

"In about eight weeks. She discovered that she was pregnant soon after she was incarcerated."

"And when will she be released?"

"Not for at least two years. Besides time served, she has to pay restitution to her victims. She has a long road ahead of her, but she promised that she would get her act together. Not only with her rehabilitation, but with being a good mother to her child when she gets out."

"Who's going to take care of the baby between now and then?"

"I am."

"You?" He looked like the last man on earth who would want a baby. He'd even said it with a horrible tone of dread. "What's going on, Tanner? Really, seriously, why would you agree to take her child?"

"Because she begged me to. And because there's no one else available to do it."

"What about the baby's father or his family?"

"The dad doesn't want anything to do with the kid and neither does his family. They're all a bunch of screwups. If I don't become its legal guardian, the baby will go into foster care."

"Then it sounds like you're doing the right thing."

"I'm trying. But all I keep thinking about is what happened to Ella."

Feeling far too emotional, Candy glanced at the lemons that had fallen on the ground and noticed that some of them were starting to brown. Ella had died from SIDS. "That's the last thing you should be thinking about."

"I know. But I can't help it."

She considered reaching out to skim his hand, to comfort him, but she refrained. The last time his life had been falling apart, she'd wrapped him in all kinds of solace, but in the end, it hadn't stopped him from pulling away. To return to that place, to feel it again, wasn't something she was willing to do.

She simply said, "It'll be okay, Tanner."

"I hope so."

"Does Meagan know if she's having a girl or a boy?"

"It's a girl." He resumed walking across the lawn. "I'm going to hire a live-in nanny. Hopefully, having someone there who knows what they're doing will make me feel better."

She walked beside him. "That's a good idea."

"I'd prefer an older lady who's already raised a brood of her own."

"Someone who knows how to be a mom?"

"Exactly."

Candy thought about how excited she'd been about becoming a mom. She also thought about the ever-present ache of losing the life in her womb. Nearly four years had passed, but she still felt the loss, especially since her miscarriage had been directly associated with her divorce.

But rather than let herself sink too deeply into those

old memories, she said, "I'm sure you'll find the right nanny." She didn't doubt he would screen them carefully.

"But first I need to find a house. The idea is for me to live in the main house with the nanny and the baby. Then later, after Meagan comes home, she and her daughter can live in the guesthouse."

By now, they were standing at the white picket fence that surrounded Candy's guesthouse. "It's nice of you to consider their future."

"I can't very well leave my sister to flounder by herself. I'm not making excuses for her, but part of the reason she embezzled money was to support her boyfriend. And then he goes off and ditches her, with a babe in her belly."

"It's probably better that he shrugged off his responsibility. She doesn't need a guy like that around."

"If I ever see his lazy ass again, I'm going to pummel the living crap out of him. It's what big brothers are supposed to do." With a tight squint, he defended his threat of violence. "He's got it coming from me."

"No doubt he does." If she were in his position, she would feel the same way. She gave him a second to clear his thoughts, then asked, "Are you ready to see the guesthouse?"

"Yes, absolutely."

She opened the gate, focusing on the sale of her property. "The tenant moved after I put it on the market, so it's vacant now. But if you decide to rent it out between now and when Meagan comes home, finding a new tenant will be easy. I've never had any trouble keeping it occupied."

"I probably wouldn't rent anything out for a while.

I've got too much else to think about." He glanced at the landscape. "You've done a great job of maintaining all of this."

"Thank you." The courtyard showcased a three-tiered fountain, next to a stretch of grass with plants and flowers. She ushered him inside. "It's one bedroom and one bath."

"I'd need to turn it into a two-bedroom."

"There's plenty of space for an addition. The people I bought it from considered making it bigger. They even looked into getting the permits."

"That's good to know."

She held back while he wandered around, letting him get a feel for it.

Afterward, he said, "It's really nice. I think Meagan would like it. But I still have to see the main house, so I'll reserve my judgment until after you show me everything."

Candy nodded. She didn't expect him to decide on the spot.

Still standing beside the window, he gazed out at the fountain. "It seems so surreal."

She knew he meant his situation, not the setting. Caught up in his reflective mood, she asked, "Has Meagan chosen a name for the baby yet?"

He turned around, the water framed behind him. "Ivy. Ivy Ann Quinn."

"That's pretty. I like the way it sounds."

"Ivy Ann is from a book about a princess Meagan read. All little girls should be princesses, right?"

"Definitely. But they don't all have to be beauty queens."

"You were Miss Teen Los Angeles when we were

going out." He said it softly, as if he were taking a romantic trip down memory lane.

To combat the gentleness in his voice, she replied, "I was always Miss Something-or-Other." Her mom had forced her into competitions at a very young age, and if Candy didn't win, she got pushed even harder. "Big bouncy hair, frozen smiles and glittery ball gowns." She winced at the image it created in her mind. "What a nightmare."

"But you still worked your tail off to make your mom proud."

"What can I say? She relished that environment. She also loved bragging about her tiara-topped daughter to her friends." To emphasize her point she made a crown-like circle with her hands, lifting it ceremoniously onto her head.

"I was guilty of bragging, too. Telling my buddies how hot my Miss Teen girlfriend was. But I shouldn't have done that, I suppose. Especially since I knew how much you hated being in those pageants."

She lowered her hands. "I hardly ever admitted that to anyone." But she'd confided in him. She'd trusted him with her secrets back then. "You were good at listening."

"And now you're listening to me talk about my problems."

"You just need to settle into the idea of being an uncle."

"I certainly never expected it to happen like this, with Meagan being a single mom." He shrugged. "But marriage doesn't make much sense to me anyway."

It shouldn't have made sense to her, either. But Candy wanted to get married again someday. She wanted to get it right next time. "Some couples are happy. Dana and Eric are."

"Then they're lucky. Because I don't think it works for most people. After Ella died, my dad had the nerve to tell my mom that he'd never loved her."

Feeling as if she'd gotten the wind knocked out of her, Candy clutched her middle. After she'd miscarried, Vince had said the same thing to her.

After a bout of silence, he said, "I'm sorry. I shouldn't be laying my mom's old troubles on you. What's done is done, and she's gone now."

Yes, his mother was gone, but Candy remained, affected by what he'd said. But before her emotions got the best of her, she lightened her mood, rather than dwell on things that couldn't be undone.

She felt especially better when Tanner glanced over and smiled. He just had that way about him.

"Ready to show me the rest of the place?" he asked.

"Yes, of course." Together, they headed for the main house, with Candy returning his smile.

Chapter Two

As the tour continued, Tanner tried to fix his attention where it should be, but he was having trouble concentrating on what Candy was saying. Something about the house being built in the 1930s? About it being a renovated bungalow with three bedrooms and two full baths?

Mostly he was noticing her. She'd always reminded him of an exotic creature, with her long-limbed agility and catlike wariness. She was beautiful, but she could be skittish, too.

They'd dated for six months. They'd been inseparable but they hadn't gone to the same high school. She'd attended an all-girls academy, an environment that made her shy around boys.

As a beauty queen, she'd hidden behind the persona she'd created. But she was different in real life. Even now, he could see fragments of the girl she'd once been: the awkward manner in which she tugged at her clothes, the way she broke eye contact.

He couldn't help but be intrigued by her. Her chestnut-colored hair was sleeker than it used to be, worn straight and falling softly to her shoulders. Her clothes were simple: a fitted T-shirt paired with black leggings—or whatever those impossibly tight things were called. Her lean, athletic shape wasn't hard to miss. And with her being a yoga instructor, he suspected she was beyond flexible. But she'd always been able to get into bendy positions. In the talent competition of the pageants, she used to perform modern dance.

The girl with the sugary name.

He used to call her all sorts of silly things: gumdrop, taffy, peanut brittle, gummy bear, lollipop. But his favorite had been cotton candy, especially when she wore pink. Did she still wear that color? Or had she outgrown it? Seventeen years had passed. A lifetime of memories.

She led him through the back door and into the kitchen, and he suspected that this was her prized room in the house, with its butcher-block island and bright white appliances. An antique cart in the corner was crowded with spices, pots and pans, old salt and pepper shakers, and other culinary knickknacks.

No doubt she liked to cook. It even smelled like cookies. It appeared as if a candle was creating the fresh-baked aroma, but it still struck him as homey, with the desired effect being the same.

She definitely seemed domestic. Even at a young age, she'd been marriage-minded. Back when they were together, she'd been determined to save herself for her future husband. She'd thought it was a romantic notion. And now she was divorced.

He wondered about the type of guy she'd married and what had gone wrong, but he sure as fire wasn't going to ask her, no matter how curious he was.

His thoughts continued to be scattered as Candy walked him all over the house, pointing out architectural details and decorative features.

Once they were in the second guestroom, she said, "This could be Ivy's nursery. It's already painted in pastels." She motioned to the walls. "Lilac trimmed in yellow."

He checked out the color theme, and she smiled, quite sweetly, as if she was picturing the baby snuggled up in this room. Seeing her expression gave him comfort, reminding him of how special she was. "Did I ever thank you for being there for me? When everything happened?"

"You were my friend. My boyfriend. I wanted to help you through it."

"I know." Behind her, the light from a set of etched glass windows was bathing the potential nursery in a warm glow. "But I just wanted to clarify that if I didn't tell you how much it meant to me then, I'm telling you now."

"You don't need to." She kept her voice soft. "Really, you don't. But I appreciate it."

"I don't want to go backward in time. But ever since Meagan asked me to become Ivy's guardian, I keep sliding into the past."

"And now, of all things, you run into me."

"It's strange, isn't it? Especially since we have a friend in common that we didn't even know about."

"Did you tell Eric that your sister is in prison and that you'll be taking care of her baby?"

He shook his head. "That wasn't something I was inclined to mention while we were getting caught up. I probably should have, though. You can tell him if you want to. You'll probably talk to him before I will. Or you'll talk to Dana or whatever."

"Does Meagan know that you've been thinking about Ella?" she asked.

"No. I couldn't say that to her. It wouldn't be right to burden her with it. And if it's crossed her mind, she hasn't said anything to me about it, either. But I think she made peace with what happened to Ella a long time ago. She talks about our sister as if she's an angel looking down on us. But maybe it's because Meagan was so young when Ella died that she saw it in a softer way."

"Kids are supposed to be more resilient."

Tanner shifted his stance, glad that Meagan didn't share his fears. "We discussed other aspects of me becoming Ivy's guardian, like how taking care of a baby is going to affect my lifestyle. I warned her that I don't know anything about being a single dad. Or any kind of dad."

"You're not the father. You're the uncle."

"Not according to tradition. In the old Cheyenne way, being an uncle is the same as being a father, and it's especially important if the dad is unavailable. In the early days, the word for *father* and *uncle* was one and the same. *Tshe-hestovestse*."

She flashed another of her sweet smiles. "That's nice. I like that."

Tanner didn't. To him, it just intensified his role in his niece's life. "I bought a bunch of baby books."

She moved a little closer. "You did?"

"Yes, but I haven't read them yet. Still, I figured it would help to know the stages and what to expect. It wouldn't be fair to Ivy to leave everything to the nanny. I don't want my niece to think I'm treating her like a leper. Babies can probably sense that kind of stuff."

"I'm sure they can." She was looking at him as if he'd just bewitched her.

Teasing her, he replied, "Is this how women are going to react to me now? Am I going to become a major chick magnet because I have a baby?"

"What are you talking about?"

"You're acting all dreamy over me, Candy."

"I am not." She got downright indignant, squaring her shoulders and jutting out her pretty little chin. "I'm just standing here."

"Making goo-goo eyes at me."

"You're full of baloney."

He shrugged, then laughed. "I was just kidding around." It was his twisted way of cracking a joke, of making light of the chemistry that still existed between them.

She made a face at him. "You always did have a rotten sense of humor."

"At least I haven't lost that side of myself. With everything that's going on, I could be crying in my beer."

"Are you kidding? You practically are."

Touché, he thought. She'd got him there. He rolled his eyes, and they both managed a genuine laugh.

He returned his attention to the pastel-colored walls, going back to where the conversation first started. "I don't know anything about decorating a nursery." He didn't have a clue about that sort of thing. "When the time comes, I'll have to get someone to help me pick out the furniture, just to be sure I don't screw it up."

"Maybe you can order a complete set, with everything already going together."

"That should work."

"It will, Tanner. It'll all work out."

"Thanks." He appreciated that she was offering positive affirmations. He needed as many good vibes as he could get. Then he took a second look at her and said, "You seem like you should've had kids. With you knowing so much about them."

She cleared her throat. "I spend a lot of time with Eric and Dana's son."

That made sense, of course. But she still seemed as if she should've had some of her own. He wondered why she hadn't, but he decided not to push the issue or pry into her personal affairs.

Next up was the master bedroom, and as soon as Candy led him to the place where she slept each night, being in the proximity of her silk-draped bed hit him square in the chest.

But why wouldn't it? Not only had they never been together in that way, he hadn't even been allowed in her room when they were kids. Her mom had been superstrict about that. But her mom wasn't part of the equation anymore. Candy and Tanner were adults now.

When their gazes locked, she began fussing with her clothes, resorting to her nervous habit. Clearly, she was feeling the heat, too.

He tried to think of something to say that would ease the tension. But nothing came to mind.

She started a choppy conversation instead, prattling

on about the room: the walk-in closet, the built-in window seat, the French door leading to the backyard.

"It produces a nice breeze," she hastily said.

"And a beautiful view," he replied, trying to glance past her and failing. Candy was the beautiful view he was talking about. He admired the way she looked, surrounded by the feminine trappings of her room. A candle was burning in here, too, like in the kitchen. Only it was something floral, a light, fluttery scent mimicking the flowers she grew in her garden. He didn't know one bee-kissed posy from another, but he remembered giving her a corsage when he'd taken her to his junior prom. But mostly what he remembered was the sweetly sinful dress she'd worn. Red, like the color of fire.

"Where do you live?" she asked suddenly.

Her question threw him off-kilter. "What?"

"You never mentioned where you live now or why you can't have the nanny and Ivy move in with you there, at least until Meagan comes home."

He snapped back to reality. "I live at the stables in a bachelor-type pad above my office. I'm going to keep it for when I need a quiet place to be alone." He quickly added, "Or to date or whatever."

"That would be better, I suppose."

"For me, it is." Curious about her future, he asked, "Are you planning on buying another house?"

She shook her head. "I wasn't going to mention this, but there's no point in hiding it. I could never afford another house. After my divorce, I bought this place with a small inheritance from my grandparents, but I got in over my head." She made a tight face. "I'm starting to fall behind on the payments on my first mortgage, and

I owe a balloon payment on my second and don't have the money for that, either."

"I'm sorry." He could see how distressing it was for her. It also explained why her ex wasn't involved. She hadn't owned the house with him.

"I'm down to a part-time job now. Enrollment is low at the studio where I work and some of my classes had to be cut. I've been looking for another part-time job to make up the difference, but I haven't found anything yet."

"I'm sorry," he said again.

"I'll get through it. Eric and Dana offered to let me stay with them after this place sells so I can take a little time to get on my feet and not burn through the money. Not that it will be that much. I messed up my equity by taking out that second loan."

"How close are you to foreclosure?"

"The bank hasn't started the proceeding yet, so there's still time. But it concerns me." She swallowed, as if a lump had formed in her throat. "I never imagined being this broke."

"I understand. I've been through some tough times, too. My mom loaned me the money for the down payment on my stables, and she took a huge risk on me. It was a run-down facility, and building it into a successful operation didn't happen overnight. It was touch-and-go there for a while. I was really worried that I was going to lose everything, including her investment in it."

"What's it like now?"

"It's everything I envisioned it should be. We offer full-service boarding, riding lessons and trails to Griffith Park. The public can rent horses from us, of course, and go on guided tours of the trails, but we also provide rentals for the movie industry. It's like the stables I worked at when I was a kid, except way nicer. We cater to both English and Western riders. We host equestrian events, too."

"It sounds wonderful. I'm glad for you, Tanner."

"Thanks. I hope things improve for you."

"For now, I just need to sell my house."

Deciding to be direct, he said, "I like this place. It has a lot going for it, but I don't know if I'm going to make an offer. I still have other properties to see."

"I understand, and I appreciate you letting me know up front. A lot of people have gushed over it, but then they disappear without a word."

"I'll let you know, either way."

"Thank you."

They exited her bedroom, and she walked him out to the porch.

Neither of them leaned forward for a hug. The emotion connected to this reunion was too heavy for a lighthearted embrace, and they both seemed to know it.

But that didn't mean he didn't hunger to take her in his arms or breathe in the scent of her skin or put his mouth against hers. If she was the kind of woman who was prone to affairs, he would seduce her, just to satisfy the longing. But he sensed that Candy wasn't that kind of woman. That deep inside, she was the same proper girl he'd left behind.

Before the moment got ridiculously quiet, he repeated his promise to keep in touch. "I'll call when I make a decision."

"Okay." Her gaze lit softly on his. "Talk to you later."

"You, too." He almost smoothed a strand of hair that blew across her cheek, but he caught himself, keeping his hands at his sides. Saying goodbye shouldn't be this hard.

He descended the steps and strode out to his truck. By the time he climbed into the cab and glanced back at the house, Candy was no longer on the porch. But it was just as well. Tanner didn't want to see her standing there, tempting him to feel things he didn't want to feel.

Later that evening, Candy sat on the sofa with her legs tucked beneath her and her smartphone on speaker. She and Dana were in the midst of a conversation, with Candy relaying the events of the day.

"Tanner seems the same, but different." A swoon-worthy boy who'd grown into a powerful man. Her heart was pounding just thinking about him. "It was a gripping reunion, that's for sure. His life is even more mixed-up than mine." She repeated his tale, going all the way back to when they were teenagers.

Dana reacted with sympathy. "That's so awful for his family, to lose a baby. And now his other sister being in prison and being forced to be separated from her child. I can't imagine how she must feel."

"You wouldn't have to imagine it. You wouldn't have embezzled money from your job. But I feel sorry for her, too. She was such a sweet little girl when I knew her."

"Tanner certainly must be a decent guy. I mean, let's face it, not many men would do what he is doing. Eric was petrified of marrying me and becoming a new father, as you well remember. And here Tanner is going to be a father figure to his niece."

"I agree that what he's doing is admirable. But he's beyond scared." Candy blew out a sigh. "He's concerned about everything, including how raising his niece over the next two years is going to affect his dating life."

"Why? Is he a player?"

"I have no idea how much he plays around." Nor did she want to envision him with a slew of women at his beck and call. "But he definitely likes being single. He made that clear. He's even keeping his apartment at the equestrian center to make dating easier. I guess he doesn't want to bring someone home to where his niece and the nanny are going to be."

Dana went silent, as if the cogs in her pretty little blond head were turning. Then she said, "Why am I getting the feeling that his dating life bothers you?"

Candy's pulse quickened. Should she admit that she was still attracted to him or keep that bit of information to herself? She opted for an evasive answer. "I don't know what you're talking about."

"Yes, you do. Come on, fess up. Give me the skinny."

She should have known better than to think she would get away with this. Fooling Dana was like trying to fool a wise old owl, even if Dana was younger than Candy. "All right, fine. There was definitely some rekindled heat between us."

"Well, thank goodness for that." A big sappy smile sounded in Dana's voice. "Do you realize that he's the first man you've been attracted to since your divorce?"

"Yes, and he's someone I used to date. Starting up with him again would be a disaster." A road that was better left untraveled.

"Maybe so, but at least you're getting your libido back."

She didn't see where that was going to help, not if it left her fantasizing about him. She needed to be careful. Because if she let her hormones drive her, she just might do something she would regret. Even now, as she touched a finger to her lips, she could conjure the long-ago flavor of his kiss.

"I think he's going to buy your house."

Distracted, Candy nearly bit the tip of her finger. She was still dreaming about the taste of Tanner's kiss. "You do? Why?"

"I just felt all along that something good would come of this."

"You always think something good will come of everything." Dana was a naturally positive person. She didn't have to try to be happy; she just was. Candy worked heart and soul to feel that kind of inner bliss. "But I hope you're right. If he buys it, then Ivy will be growing up in my house, and that's a nice thought. I also like the idea of it becoming the place Meagan shares with her daughter."

But what about Tanner? she asked herself.

How did she feel about him being part of the mix? Did she want him—this beautifully complicated man from her past—drinking coffee in her kitchen or showering in her tub or sleeping in her room?

Yes, heaven help her, she did. As romantically frazzled as her connection to him was, Candy was intrigued by the notion of Tanner living there, too.

Chapter Three

The sun shined in the sky, reminiscent of the happy drawings Meagan used to do. But the crayon-colored weather didn't improve the setting, and neither did the other families gathered on picnic-style benches. The chain-link fence and watchful eyes of prison guards ruined it. As much as Tanner loved his sister, he hated visiting her here.

Struggling not to frown, he glanced across their bench, where she sat attired in her unflattering uniform. Meagan was a level-one inmate, which meant that she was the least dangerous kind of offender. At the moment, she was considered special needs because of her pregnancy.

But she wasn't glowing, the way an expectant mother should. Shadows dogged her eyes, and her long dark hair hung limply down her back. She kept her hand on her swollen belly, rubbing it from time to time.

Was she trying to comfort Ivy? Her due date was two months from now, and providing there were no complications, she would be allowed to stay in the hospital twenty-four to forty-eight hours after giving birth, before the baby would be taken away and Meagan would be returned to the prison population.

Tanner wished that he didn't know so much about the system or about how newborns were brought into it. He wished his sister had never committed a crime and that he wasn't beholden to help raise her child. But that was the way it was, and he had to learn to cope with it.

"I found two houses that I'm considering," he said. "I just need to make a decision between them, and I don't know which one to pick."

"The choice is yours." She sounded cautious about caring too much, as if it was too far in the future for her to grasp. "It's going to be your house."

"It'll be yours and Ivy's, too." And he wanted her to feel as if she was part of the process. "I didn't take any pictures. I should have, but I just got so overwhelmed with it all."

"It's okay. Just choose the house you like best."

Trying to stir a better reaction out of her, he said, "The first one is on a really nice piece of property with a flower garden, a big green lawn and fruit trees. The guesthouse in the back has its own yard. It even has a fountain."

She leaned forward, her interest piqued. "That sounds pretty."

He thought about the owner and how pretty she was, too. "It's weird, though, because it belongs to an old girlfriend of mine."

Her eyebrows shot up. "Since when did you have a girlfriend? I thought you just..."

Screwed around? He decided not to fill in the blank. It was already perfectly clear as to what she meant. "It's Candy, from when I was a teenager. I'm not sure if you remember her, but you liked her when you were a kid. In fact, you more or less idolized her."

Meagan laughed a little. "Of course I remember her. She was like Miss America or something. Mom used to talk about her all the time. There are even some pictures of the two of you in one of those old photo albums Mom put together. I paged through them after Mom died."

"I didn't know there were pictures of us around." But he hadn't gone through the albums. He wasn't keen on reminiscing. Of course he'd been doing it since he'd run into Candy, letting his mind stray in all sorts of directions.

Meagan's voice cut into his thoughts. "As far I could tell they were from a school dance."

When Candy had worn the red dress? Now he was curious to see them, to refresh his memory about that night in greater detail, but he wasn't about to go digging through the storage shed where Meagan kept their mother's belongings. He missed his mom, but being around her things didn't give him comfort, the way it did for his sister. "If they're from a school dance, then it must be my junior prom. That's the only dance we went to. So, how did we look?"

"She looked like she just stepped out of a magazine."

He didn't doubt it. He'd been wildly proud to show her off, introducing her to anyone she hadn't met before. "And what about me?"

"Are you kidding? You looked like a total goof."

"Gee, thanks." He rolled his eyes. "Spoken like a true sister."

Meagan shrugged. "I wanted to grow up to be just like her." She twisted her stringy hair. "Did I accomplish it? Is she a mess these days, too?"

"She's still beautiful, and so are you."

"Spoken like a true brother." She glanced away, heavy with emotion. "A lying brother." She returned her gaze to his, still resting a hand on her stomach. "Does Candy have kids?"

"No." He noticed how many children were visiting their loved ones in this awful environment, though, and every time he brought Ivy back here to see Meagan, it would be a constant reminder that his niece would be one of them.

"So, she's not married or anything?"

"She's divorced." From the husband he wondered about. The man who'd become the mystery Tanner shouldn't care about solving. To keep Meagan from asking more personal, Candy-related questions, he went back to discussing the real-estate purchase. "The only concern I have is that her guesthouse isn't big enough. It's only one bedroom, so I'd have to hire a contractor to add another one."

"Is that a major ordeal?"

"Candy said getting the permits wouldn't be a problem."

"Would the addition cost a lot of money?"

"That depends, I guess, on how you evaluate it. The other house I'm considering has a two-bedroom guesthouse already on it. But the overall price of the property is more."

"So it balances out the same?"

He nodded.

"Tell me about the other house and what you like about that one."

"Besides the guesthouse? It's less maintenance. It wouldn't require as much yard work. It's newer, too. But it doesn't have the charm, either. The guesthouse on Candy's property has that storybook-type architecture."

"Like the magic cottages in the stories Mom used to read to me?" She sighed, behaving like the dreamy kid she used to be. "I loved those stories. I'm going to read them to Ivy, too."

His heart clawed its way to his throat. "Maybe I should buy Candy's place."

She snapped out of her gentle musings. "You don't have to do that for me. Like I said before, you should choose the one you like best."

"Truthfully, I don't have a preference. I'd rather choose it for you and Ivy, and I think Candy's place would suit you and your daughter." The other house seemed dull by comparison. "I could see Ivy running around in the yard when she's a little older, darting through the flowers and trees."

"Oh, that's sweet. I like that."

"I like it, too."

"Thank you, Tanner. For everything you're doing for me and my baby."

"Just keep your promise about staying on the straight and narrow, and we'll be fine."

"I will. And what I said about you looking like a goof in the pictures with Candy wasn't true. You were as handsome as always, and the two of you made a cute couple."

"Don't worry about it. How I looked back then is of no consequence now. Nor is the type of couple Candy and I used to be. All I'm doing is buying her house, not getting involved with her again."

"Don't you want to at least be friends with her?"

Did he? "I don't know. Having a past with someone is complicated."

"Mom used to say that Candy was good for you."

Cripes, he thought. Did that have to keep surfacing? Wasn't it enough that he'd already told Candy how his mom had felt? "You remember her saying that?"

"I remember her saying all sorts of things. She went on about the same stuff for years. But I didn't mind. I liked that Mom trusted me enough to say what was on her mind. It made me feel more grown-up."

Everyone was grown-up now, he thought, including him and Candy. Was he was wrong about the complication of being friends? If living in her house eased his mind, then wouldn't having her as a friend do the same thing? Maybe his mom wasn't so far off the mark about Candy being good for him.

And maybe he was grasping at straws, using his old girlfriend as the baby buffer. With Ivy's impending arrival creeping up on him, he was obviously too confused to know what to think.

Meagan shifted in her seat, a breeze riffling her shirt and pulling it closer to her oversize bump.

"What are you thinking about?" she asked.

"Nothing." He didn't doubt that she was as scared as he was, maybe even more so. She was having a child that she was barely going to know. He reached across the table, encouraging her to take his hand. His jailbird sister and the little person in her womb.

* * *

Dana was right, Candy thought. Tanner was going to buy her house. He'd made an offer on the phone, and they'd discussed the price and the terms, and now he was coming over to bring a written copy of the agreement and a check for the deposit.

As much as she was going to miss her beloved home, she was happy about the sale. It gave her comfort to know that he and Ivy and Meagan would be the family associated with it.

Still, for her, starting over somewhere else was a daunting thought. But, she reminded herself, she would be staying with Dana and Eric for as long as she needed their help, and their generosity was a godsend, a much-needed opportunity to get her finances in order before she ventured back out on her own.

When the doorbell rang, signaling Tanner's arrival, she calmly answered it. This time, she wasn't going to overreact to her attraction to him.

He was dressed in street clothes instead of riding gear, but that didn't detract from his appeal. Those slate-gray eyes bore straight into hers, giving her a sexy shiver.

So much for not overreacting.

Was she affecting him in a sexy way, too? Even though her appearance was something she downplayed, she wanted him to notice her. A double-edged sword, she thought, as he entered the house and made her heart go bump. Her newfound libido was getting in the way.

But there were other factors involved, too, like the way her ex used to react to her. Vince was a photographer, and he was always critiquing the angles of her face or the lines of her body. Her mom was notorious for that, too. But not Tanner. He'd never told her how to look or act or feel. Mostly, he'd just smiled his approval.

Like now.

Her heart bumped again, and she offered him a seat at the dining room table. He gave her that body-warming smile, and she noticed that he had a manila envelope in his hand.

"Where's Yogi?" he asked.

"She's on a playdate with a friend."

His smile shifted to a sideways grin. "Your pet lives a cool life."

She warned herself to get down to business. Either that or make Tanner her pet, too. "Before I look over the paperwork, can I get you anything? Coffee, tea, water, juice?"

"Coffee sounds good. I take it black."

She headed to the kitchen and brewed a single cup for him and tea for herself. She decided to put some muffins on a platter, too, arranging them just so.

Candy enjoyed being a hostess. One of the things she would miss most about her house was the parties she used to have here, particularly the outdoor gatherings. She'd designed her yard for entertaining guests, creating a homey atmosphere. She hoped Tanner would make good use of it, too.

She brought everything to the table. He thanked her for the coffee and took a sip.

She sat next to him. "Would you like a muffin? They're orange spice and oatmeal. I baked them last night. They're made from whole-grain flour." She'd also put applesauce in the batter to keep them moist. "It's a healthy recipe."

"Sure. I'll try one. So you're the natural-food type? I

remember when you used to eat french fries and drink milk shakes."

"I still indulge in junk food now and then, but mostly I try to eat healthy. I'm a vegetarian now."

"That doesn't surprise me. You never liked burgers. You used to wince when I ordered mine rare."

She winced accordingly, and he smiled once again. Mercy, she thought. A young, handsome, wealthy bachelor, soon to have an infant in tow. He'd been right about being a chick magnet. Even his fear of raising the baby would probably work in his favor. She didn't doubt that women would be clamoring to come to his emotional rescue.

Was Candy turning into one of those women?

To keep herself from making goo-goo eyes at him—something he'd accused her of doing the last time he was here—she reached for the envelope he'd left on the table.

She opened it, and he bit into a muffin. He drank more of his coffee, too.

After she read the four-page purchase agreement, Tanner handed her the check for the deposit, and they both signed the paperwork. Everything they'd discussed was in there.

She said, "I'll open an escrow account first thing in the morning." It was too late to do it today. But once it was done, the escrow office would handle the rest of it, representing and protecting both parties involved. Candy had been through this before, only last time she'd been the buyer. Still, she understood the process.

He finished the muffin. "This is really good, by the way."

"Thanks." She was glad that he was enjoying the snack she'd made.

He reached for another muffin and broke it in half, dropping crumbs onto his napkin. "I saw Meagan this weekend, and she helped me decide between this place and another one. I described your guesthouse to her, but I also told her that I could see Ivy running around in your yard. It was a nice image for both of us."

It warmed her soul to hear it. So much so, she wanted to lift her hand to his jaw and feel the masculine warmth of his skin. But she didn't, of course.

Keeping things light, she said, "I wonder if Ivy will look like Meagan. She was such a cute kid."

"She remembers you, how gorgeous she thought you were and how much she wanted to be like you. She even mentioned that there are some pictures of you and me in an old photo album. From what she said about them, I'm guessing they're from my junior prom."

Suddenly Candy felt seventeen again, or as close to it as a thirty-four-year-old could get. "That was a fun night." Happy and starry and romantic.

"From what I can remember, your dress was red and the front of it was…" He made a curved motion.

She was surprised that he recalled something so specific. But she had a vivid recollection of it, too. "That was the first time I didn't mind wearing a ball gown." Because she hadn't been gliding across a stage, being judged for her poise and grace. "It had a sweetheart neckline. That's a popular design."

"It looked spectacular on you. It revealed just enough cleavage to drive a poor boy like me wild. I think my tongue was lolling out of my mouth. When I wasn't sticking it down your throat."

Feeling far too free, she laughed. "The perils of youth."

He laughed, too. "I called you Red Hots that night, after those spicy little red candies."

"I was always some sort of candy to you."

"The perils of your name."

She smiled. "So it seems."

"You really did look hot in that sweetheart dress."

"It was certainly our fanciest date." She hadn't taken him to her junior prom because she'd had a pageant the same day, and those competitions had always come first. She hadn't gone to her senior one for the very same reason. But by then, she and Tanner had broken up. Curious, she asked, "What was your other prom like?"

"What other prom?"

"Your senior one. Did you go? Was it everything it was supposed to be?"

"It was okay, I guess. I took a girl who was the party type, but that's what I was into by then. Mostly we got drunk and passed out in the hotel room all of us had rented."

"All of you?"

"The group I went with. It wasn't a lone date, like yours and mine. And if it's any consolation, I had a horrible hangover the next day. Oh, and I got cussed out by my dad. I don't remember what it was about. I just remember him yelling at me over the phone."

Candy barely knew Tanner's father. He'd traveled for work and was hardly ever home. But when he was there, she'd noticed how the family had to jump to his tune. Obviously, it had only gotten worse after the divorce. "You're going to be better with Ivy than he was with any of you."

"I'm sure as hell going to try. Maybe I can get some pointers from Eric. He'll understand the father/uncle thing. It's probably the same in his tribe."

"When do you plan to talk to him?"

"I don't know. But I'd like to meet Dana, too."

She had a brainstorm. "I can arrange for the four of us to get together. Maybe I can have a barbecue here next Sunday, if everyone is available. They can bring Jude, their son, so you can get used to being around a baby. Or a toddler, in his case. He's around fifteen months. But he's still within the age range that Ivy will be while she'll be under your care."

"That sounds great. I agree that it might take a little pressure off me to be around their son. I don't know anyone else who has a baby."

"I'll call them tonight, and if they can come, then I'll text you and let you know what time to be here on Sunday."

"Sounds like a plan. I can bring some steaks for us meat eaters to toss on the grill, if that's okay."

"Dana and Eric are both meat eaters, so I was going to provide something for the carnivores, but if you want to do it, I don't mind. I'll make plenty of salads and side dishes." She paused to think about what was in store for her. "If this barbecue happens, it'll be my last hurrah." Her final party at the house. "As soon as it's over, I'll have to start packing and putting things in storage. That thirty-day escrow is going to smack me upside the head if I'm not ready for it."

"And that baby is going to knock me upside mine if I'm not ready for her." He stood up, ending the visit. "Hopefully I'll see all of you on Sunday."

Candy came to her feet, as well. "I hope so, too." She

wanted to say goodbye to her house in a festive way, but she also wanted to make things easier for Tanner, giving him and Ivy a chance to flourish here.

Chapter Four

On the day of the barbecue, Tanner went to the market and picked up three porterhouse steaks. While he was at the store, he considered a hostess gift for Candy.

Maybe an assortment of candy in honor of his old nicknames for her? No, that wouldn't do. She was too much of a healthy eater now. Besides, he didn't want to make this about the past.

A bottle of wine? He shook his head. She might not even be serving alcohol at this get-together.

A bouquet of flowers? That didn't seem right, either. She could pick flowers from her yard and put them in a vase if she wanted to. How about a potted plant, instead? Once again, he nixed it. A plant would be in the way while she was in transition from the move.

Finally it hit him: seeds. She could plant them when she was resettled and ready to start a new garden. Flowers, fruits, herbs, whatever he could find.

Pleased with the idea, he paid for the steaks, then checked his phone and located a nursery. Luckily, it was only a few blocks away.

He drove there, parked his truck and went into the main building, where he found an impressive display of seed packets. He selected them at random, hoping to get a nice variety.

He looked around and noticed a gift bag, already equipped with a bow, so he grabbed that, as well. Once he paid for everything, he put the seeds in the bag, ready to see Candy.

On his way to her house, he wondered if they were becoming friends, if this was the start of something new and fresh. And if it was, how would it affect the heat between them? Would their attraction get in the way? Or would they be able to rein it in?

By the time he turned onto her street and parked his truck, he was as confused as ever, unsure of what to expect when he was around her. But he wasn't going to let it bog down his brain. Part of the reason she'd arranged the barbecue was to help him get comfortable in an environment where a baby was involved, and he was determined to do that.

He didn't see Eric's, car so he assumed that he and Dana weren't here yet. There were quite a few other vehicles parked on the street, though. This was the type of neighborhood with lots of activity, especially on weekends.

After exiting his truck, he gathered his purchases, climbed the porch steps and noticed that the front door was open. Was that an invitation to enter without ringing the bell?

Splitting the difference, he knocked on the door

frame, then poked his head in and called out, "It's Tanner."

No one replied. But maybe Candy was in the backyard, setting things up.

He stepped inside and Yogi came around the corner and flashed her big brown eyes. An untrained dog would have run out the door and down the street. This one obviously knew her boundaries.

"Hey, girl," he said. "Where's your mistress?"

She turned and looked in the direction of the kitchen.

Impressed, Tanner patted her head. It was like talking to Lassie. "Thanks. I'll go on in there and give her the steaks I brought." Yogi sniffed the market bag, and Tanner smiled. "I'll give you some of mine after it's cooked, if you're allowed table scraps."

On his way to the kitchen, he put the gift bag on the dining room table. He would give it to Candy in a little while, rather than hand it to her right away.

Upon entering the kitchen, he saw her at the counter, shucking corn. The butcher-block island was filled with food she'd already fixed: a relish platter, potato salad, diced fruit, cheese and crackers, chips, dips.

She was facing the window with her back to him. She was also listening to a music device that was clipped to her clothes and plugged into her ears.

She danced while she worked. A soft sway of her hips. The song must have been light and easy. He could have watched her all day. She was wearing a fitted top, khaki shorts and sandals. The bareness of her legs left him wanting more.

More skin. More of everything.

Guilty, he glanced around for the dog. Sure enough, Yogi was observing him while he admired Candy. Tanner made a sheepish expression. It was bad enough that he couldn't control his attraction to her, let alone getting caught by a Labrador.

"Go tell her I'm here," he said, making a motion he had no doubt the dog would understand.

Yogi did exactly what he asked and went over to Candy and nudged her leg.

Candy turned and spotted him, removing the buds from her ears. "Oh, my goodness. How long have you been there?"

"Not long." Tanner tried to behave as if he hadn't been ogling her. Thank goodness the dog couldn't talk. "The door was open. I assumed it was okay."

"It's totally okay. But I lost track of time." She glanced at the microwave clock.

He glanced at the clock, too. It was 2:11. The invitation was for two. "When do you think Eric and Dana are going to get here?"

She dusted the corn silk from her fingers. "They called a while ago and said they were going to be late. They wanted to be sure that Jude got his nap before they brought him over. Otherwise he gets more hyper than he already is."

Jude was the kid who was supposed to make the baby thing easier, but he was starting to sound like a holy terror.

"He's always into something," Candy continued. "Perpetual motion, like his mother. But you're going to adore him. Everyone does."

Tanner decided he would just have to wait and see. He held up the market bag. "I brought the steaks. I promised Yogi a few bites of mine if she's allowed."

"She is, and I'm sure she'll be eternally grateful. She doesn't understand my tofu ways."

"Can't say as I blame her." He looked at Yogi. She was dividing her gaze between him and Candy, watching them like a tennis match. He lifted the steaks a little higher. "Is it all right if I put these in the fridge?"

"Oh, here, let me do it." She came forward and reached for the bag. "Where are my manners, just leaving you standing there like that?"

He didn't mind standing there, as long she was nearby. He gestured to the center island. "Everything looks great."

"Thanks. Making party food is fun." She put away the steaks. "If you're hungry, you can snack while we're waiting for Eric and Dana."

"That's okay. I can wait." The chips and dip were tempting, though. He was a sucker for guacamole, the spicier the better, and he suspected hers would have a nice little kick.

Still at the fridge, she asked, "How about some lemonade? It's freshly squeezed."

"Courtesy of the tree in the yard? I have no idea what I'm going to do with all of those lemons after I move in. Maybe I'll bag them up and bring them to you."

She poured him a glass. "I'd be glad to take them. I have a slew of recipes that involve lemons."

He accepted the drink. "I don't do much cooking. I plan to rely on the nanny for that. But I guess I'll have to learn to fix a few meals when Ivy is old enough to eat solid food." He shrugged, smiled. "To keep her from starving on the nanny's days off."

She smiled, too. "It's easy to cook for little kids."

"Unless Ivy turns out to be a picky eater."

"Is Meagan a picky eater?"

"My sister is a picky everything. No, wait, strike that. She has no discretion when it comes to men." Rather than get worked up about the baby's deadbeat dad, he abruptly said, "I brought you a little something."

"You did?"

"I left it on the dining table. I'll go get it."

He grabbed the gift bag, came back and handed it to her.

"This is lovely," she said, looking at the bag.

"It came like that." A floral design, topped with a curlicue bow. "I can't take credit for it."

She opened the bag and uncovered the seed packages. "Oh, Tanner, these are perfect. Thank you."

"I figured you could plant them when the time felt right. I imagine you'll want to have a garden at the next place you live."

"I definitely will. Eric and Dana have a garden in their backyard that was inspired by mine. I can enjoy theirs while I'm staying with them, but I can't stay there forever. I'll need to create new roots for myself." She sorted through the seeds. "I wonder what these combinations mean."

"Mean?"

"Just about every plant or flower has a meaning. It's called floriography. In the Victorian era, people used to communicate through the bouquets they exchanged. They used flower-language dictionaries to help them decipher the codes. I just started learning about it, and I've been thinking about planting my next garden that way, by grouping specific plants and flowers together to create messages."

"That sounds fascinating. I like that idea."

"Not all of the dictionaries were the same. Some flowers had several different meanings, depending on what dictionary was being used."

"That could get confusing."

"I suspect that some of the messages were deciphered incorrectly." She studied the seed packages again. "I have a book about floriography. Should I look these up?"

"Sure." Why not? He couldn't begin to guess what sort of code would be unmasked. "I chose them randomly, so who knows what will surface?"

"The book is over there." She headed for the antique cart in the corner. "I think it's on the bottom shelf." She bent down and scanned a grouping of books. "Here it is."

Before she got started, he asked, "Will you look up the ivy plant and see if it's in there?" He couldn't help but wonder about the name Meagan had picked for her daughter.

Candy went straight to a glossary in the back. "Let's see. Oh, here we go. Ivy. The first sentiment is 'wedded love.' But it also means 'friendship.'"

He made a face. "Talk about a contradiction in terms. A man sends a woman a wreath of ivy because he regards her as a friend, and she assumes that he wants to marry her."

She laughed a little. "That would be a disaster. But I prefer 'wedded love.' Most women would, I suppose."

Most marriage-minded women, he thought, and apparently some divorced ones, too. He was already curious about her failed marriage, and now it was driven even deeper into his mind. But why wouldn't it be, especially after the importance she'd placed all those years ago on being some future guy's wife?

She shook the seed packet of a flowering shrub and said, "Let's see what this means." After checking the glossary, she pursed her lips. "It says, 'I am dangerous.'"

"Is that supposed to apply to you or to me?"

"To you. The person giving the plant." She searched his gaze, her eyes locking onto his. "So, are you, Tanner?"

Dangerous? A man capable of creating peril? How was he supposed to respond to something like that? "I guess it depends on how you define it."

"Maybe we shouldn't try to figure it out. Maybe it's better to just take it at face value."

And assume that he was? "What do the rest of the seeds mean?" Mundane things, he hoped. He didn't like feeling that his character was on the line.

She went back to the book. "The next one is 'protection from danger.'" Her voice turned light. "Oh, my goodness, how funny is that?"

Oddly funny. But he was grateful for the reprieve. "First I tell you I'm dangerous, then I offer you protection from danger. I'm quite a guy."

"You certainly have a way with floriography."

"So it seems."

"Should I keep going?" she asked.

"You might as well." He was too curious to stop now.

Again, she consulted the book. "Now you're asking me to dance."

"I am?"

"Yes. It says, 'Will you dance with me?'"

"I saw you dancing by yourself earlier."

Her cheeks flushed. "That was embarrassing."

"I thought you looked cute. And there's no need to be embarrassed around me. I've seen you dance by yourself before."

She gave him a pointed look. "Performing on stage is different from assuming that you're alone in your kitchen."

He shrugged, trying to get himself off the hook. "As long as we're talking dances, do you remember what kind of flowers that were on the corsage I gave you when I took you to the prom?"

"Yes, I remember. A girl doesn't forget the first time a boy gives her a corsage." She glanced at her wrist, as if the ornament was still there. "It was a white carnation with baby's breath."

"And what do those mean?"

She checked the glossary. "White carnations symbolize innocence." After a slight pause, she added, "That's what baby's breath means, too."

"Go figure. A dangerous boy and an innocent girl." He was beginning to enjoy these messages, to see them in a whole new way. "Maybe there is something to this flower-language stuff."

She closed the book with a soft whoosh, fluttering its pages. "You're only saying that because I got stuck with the innocent mantle."

"Would you rather have a wild mantle?" He waggled his eyebrows. "Just tell me what flower symbolizes a wanton woman, and I'll give you one of those the next time I take you dancing."

"You aren't taking me anywhere, smarty."

"According to the floriography, I already asked you to dance." He bowed like a gentleman caller who was going to waltz her around the kitchen.

She laughed. "Go use your charms on someone else."

"Don't be hasty." Still bent at the waist, he peered up at her. "Have you forgotten my offer of protection?"

"From the dangerous cad that you are?" She moved away from him. "I think it's time for me to finish cleaning the corn."

"Sure. Go ahead. Just let me suffer here alone."

She rolled her eyes and returned to the sink. "I'm sure you'll survive."

All jokes aside, now he wanted to take her dancing. He wanted to sweep her off to bed, too, to lose himself in her innocence or wildness or whatever role she chose to play. Of course, he'd already surmised that she wasn't the play-around type. That didn't stop him from wishing otherwise, though.

Now Tanner needed a diversion, something to take his mind off doing bad things to her. "I think I'll grab some chips and dip."

He prepared a plate and stood off to the side, trying to clear the sexual toxins from his pores. But it didn't work. The spices in the guacamole were as sizzling as he'd assumed they would be, making his blood hotter.

She went back to the corn, leaving him to his own devices. He drank the rest of his lemonade, wishing he could douse himself with it instead.

Luckily, Eric and Dana and their son soon arrived, and Tanner gladly redirected his focus.

He and Eric shook hands, and introductions were made. Dana said hello and offered a big smile. She was a shapely blonde who appeared to be in her mid-to-late twenties, whereas Eric was in his forties. Tanner hadn't expected an age difference. But it didn't matter. They looked natural together.

As for Jude, he was a cute little pistol, with his father's Native coloring and his mother's bright blue eyes. He squirmed and laughed and tried to leap out of Dana's arms to get to Candy.

"Canny!" he squealed in his toddler speak.

"Jude!" she replied with equal enthusiasm and reached for him. Just as quickly, he was looped around her, puckering up for a kiss. *Smack. Smack.* The exchange was deliberately loud and admirably sweet.

"He adores her," Dana said with pride.

Tanner merely nodded. He couldn't seem to stop watching them. Jude rested his head against Candy's shoulder and flashed a set of devilish dimples. In that cozy instant, Tanner wondered, once again, why she hadn't had kids of her own. But mostly he wondered about her ex and why their marriage had gone south.

"Is everyone ready to barbecue?" Candy asked, adjusting the imp in her arms.

"Yes, let's do it," Dana replied, reaching for a platter.

Eric helped carry the food, too. He also offered to fire up the grill, and he and his wife went outside together. Yogi followed them out the door. Somewhere between the floriography and Eric's family arriving, Tanner had lost track of the dog.

And now he and Candy were alone in the kitchen with the other couple's child. Jude was still nuzzled against her shoulder, using it like a pillow.

The boy cocked his head and pointed to Tanner. "You?"

"Me?"

"He wants to know your name," Candy said.

Tanner cleared his throat. He didn't know how to have a conversation with a toddler. Too many years had passed since Meagan was little, and as vivid as his memories about Ella were, she was too young to have started talking before she died.

He gave it his best shot. "I'm Tanner."

"Tanny," the boy replied.

Canny for Candy, and Tanny for him. Was Jude lumping them together in his young mind? Should he correct him?

Tanner looked to Candy for help. But she was biting back a grin, as if she thought it was funny. He was outnumbered. He'd probably been outsmarted, too. For all he knew, Jude was a prodigy who could speak like a scholar.

The three of them went outside to join Eric and Dana, and the barbecue got under way.

Eric cooked the steaks. He also placed the tofu kebabs Candy had fixed for herself on the grill.

When they sat down to eat, Jude reached for his mother, then his father, then went back to Candy, taking turns on each adult's lap. Tanner was getting dizzy just watching him. It was like musical chairs without the music.

As he watched the scene unfold, he felt slighted that he'd been left out. Yet he was relieved, too. He had mixed emotions about being part of Jude's hold-me circle. He wasn't sure if he could've handled it. But that didn't stop him from analyzing every move the little tyke made.

Jude nibbled from his mom's plate. He even ate bits of tofu off of Candy's. But his favorite activity was squeezing pieces of fruit between his fingers.

When Jude caught Tanner watching him, the kid

perked to attention and extended both hands, offering him globs of mashed-up watermelon.

"He doesn't want that, sweetie," his mother quickly said, taking the mess away from him.

Jude stuck out his lower lip, and even though he didn't cry, Tanner felt bad. To make up for it, he squished up some of the fruit on his own plate and showed it to Jude. For an encore, Tanner popped a grape into the air and let it land on the table, before pouncing on it with his thumb.

The boy broke into a belly laugh and clapped.

"See?" Eric said to Tanner with a laugh much tamer than his son's. "You're already getting the hang of this."

"I'm getting the hang of causing trouble." But it felt good to score points. He wiped his hands on his napkin while Dana attempted to clean Jude's. Since Tanner was on a roll, he said, "I promised Yogi some of my steak." He turned to Candy. "Can I feed her here at the table?"

She nodded and smiled, and he suspected that she was impressed with the way he'd mimicked Jude's squishy fruit antics. It didn't take much to please this crowd.

Tanner cut up treat-size bites of his steak and called Yogi over to the table. The dog had been waiting patiently. Jude craned his neck to watch, applauding every time the dog caught a bite. Yogi preened under the attention. Tanner knew just how she felt.

After everyone had finished their meal, Eric went out to his vehicle to get a mini-playpen or travel crib or whatever they were referred to as these days. He set it up in the shade, unfolding it easily.

It was a pretty cool contraption, and Jude seemed excited to see it. In he went, with a boatload of toys.

"I'm going to have to get one of those," Tanner said.

"You're going to have to get lots of stuff," Dana assured him with her twentysomething smile.

"I can shop with you," Candy said, sounding like the friend she was fast becoming.

Grateful for the offer, he said, "That would be great." It made him feel less alone, less intimidated by his future plight. "But we'll have to wait until I move in here."

"Did you know I used to live here?" Dana asked. She gestured to the guesthouse. "I was one of Candy's tenants."

"My very best tenant," Candy put in.

Eric interjected, "It's where Dana lived when we started dating."

His wife shot him a sly glance. "By dating, he means it's where I lived when we had our one-night stand that produced Jude."

Eric shook his head, but he laughed, too. "Dana has no filter. She just says whatever is on her mind. I've gotten used to it by now."

Tanner glanced at the guesthouse, then at Jude, who was tossing his toys against the side of his cage. The little hellion had been conceived on this property?

Dana said, "Eric and I met at the diner where I work. I'm a waitress, but I've been studying all sorts of things in school. I can't decide what I'm going to be when I grow up."

Tanner doubted that she was ever going to grow up, but that was part of her charm. "I have a degree in business. It was one of those general choices that seemed to fit."

"I have a degree in riding around in convertibles in parades," Candy said, making a crack about her beauty-queen days. After mimicking a robotic wave, she added, "I can bat my eyelashes, too."

"I never minded when you batted them at me," Tanner told her.

She ducked her head, and he realized that he'd just flirted with her, and in front of Eric and Dana, no less. He couldn't backpedal, so he shot her a wicked smile, reminding her that he was the dangerous guy, and she was the innocent girl.

Dana watched the exchange with far too much interest, making the moment more obvious.

"Where did you two meet?" she asked.

Tanner waited for Candy to reply, but she merely smiled. He smiled, too, more softly this time. Then he said, "It was at the bowling alley down the street from where I used to live. I was there by myself, killing time. It was a weekday, after school, and I was bored out of my mind." He added more detail, more memory. "I'd gone there with the intention to play pool, to act all tough and brooding like a hustler, but the billiards tables were full, so I decided to bowl instead."

"That's not nearly as sexy," Dana said, shooting him a silly smirk.

He chuckled. "Yeah, but I was a slick bowler, if I do say so myself."

Candy finally chimed in. "And guess who was in the lane next to him?" She answered her own question. "Proper, well-behaved me, of course. But I wasn't alone. I wasn't with a group of friends, either. I was with my grandparents."

Dana laughed, shoving her thick blond hair away from her face. "Talk about teenage mortification."

Tanner leaned back in his chair. "I didn't care who

she was with. She was the most beautiful girl I'd ever seen, and I couldn't keep my eyes off her."

Candy blew out her breath, as if she was reliving the feeling. "He was making me so nervous, I kept flubbing up and getting gutter balls."

Tanner finished the story. "Her grandpa finally told me to just ask for her dang number and quit screwing up her game."

Eric jumped into the conversation. "Grandpa sounded like a cool guy."

"Sometimes he was grumpy," Candy said. "But he was always there for me. I miss him and Grandma."

"They seemed to like me," Tanner said. "But her mother didn't." He asked Candy, "Does she know I'm buying your house?"

She shook her head. "No. I haven't told her yet."

"I wonder what she'll think."

"I don't know. But I'm sure she'll have something to say about it."

No doubt, Tanner thought. Her mom was highly critical and snidely opinionated. Her name was Jonelle, but people called her Jo. He'd always figured that Candy had gotten her gentle personality from her father, even if she'd never really known him. As for her looks, he assumed that gene had come from her dad, too. Jo wasn't an attractive woman.

Candy stood up and moved away from the table. "There's homemade pudding in the fridge if anyone wants some."

Just like that, the mother conversation ended. But it was just as well. There was no point in making this about Jo.

Jude squealed when the pudding was served. It

started off fine, with Dana feeding it to him, but then he tried to take the spoon away from her and do it himself. Clearly, he wasn't old enough to have acquired those skills and the pudding went everywhere.

Somehow, it turned into a game. No temper tantrums, just lots of giggles. Halfway through the bowl, his face was covered in tapioca. He had it in his hair and on his clothes, too. The bib he was wearing barely helped.

His parents joined forces, cleaning him up and dressing him in a new outfit. Changing his wet diaper was part of the ordeal, but Jude didn't want to hold still for any of it. He kicked his feet and eyeballed Tanner, as if calling upon his partner in crime to misbehave, too.

The party wound down, and a fresh and sparkling Jude made his way onto Tanner's lap. Out of the blue, the kid decided to hug him. Caught by surprise, he returned the embrace and nuzzled the boy's fluffy hair.

It was sweet and tender, making him feel as if he'd just scaled a mountain. Only when Jude pulled away and he could no longer feel the boy's heartbeat tapping warmly against his own, Tanner went into fear mode. He reached out trying to keep Jude there, but the child toddled off, leaving Tanner much too alone.

Chapter Five

After Eric and his family left, Tanner helped Candy clean up. She had no idea what he was thinking or feeling, but she was rife with emotion. She'd seen the way he'd wrapped his arms around Jude, the warm expression on his face while he'd brushed his cheek against her godson's hair. She'd also noticed how lost he'd seemed when Jude had run away from him. But she wasn't sure how to broach it, so she started with casual dialogue.

"Thanks for helping me out," she said, as they put leftovers away in the kitchen.

"It's the least I can do, considering you hosted this get-together with me in mind."

"It was fun. I enjoyed it." She paused to deliver her next line, hoping to ease him into a deeper conversation. "You were certainly a hit with Jude."

"He's a cool kid. It did take some of the pressure off to be around him. But it added some pressure, too."

The opening she'd been waiting for. "How so?"

"Seeing how active he is, for one thing. You warned me that he was in perpetual motion, and you were right. That little dude never stops going. I got worn-out just watching him."

"It was sweet when he hugged you." There. She'd said it. She'd brought it up.

"It was sweet," he agreed. "So damned sweet. But just when I was getting used to holding him, when it felt good and right, he was gone."

"All Jude did was run off to play."

"I know. But it still affected me in a weird way. I wish I could go back to being the guy I used to be. No responsibility, no one to take care of but myself."

The sans-baby bachelor? "You can't be that guy anymore." She handed him the potato salad. "Ivy needs you."

"I'm going to try to do right by her. I swear I am." He turned away to face the counter to dump the mixture into a plastic container. "But I'm just so out of my element." He paused. "Maybe I should go on a binge before Ivy is born. Maybe I should get raging drunk and have tons of sex."

She stared at his broad back. He'd gone from babies to sex in ten seconds flat. "With who?"

He didn't turn around. "With anyone who wants to join me."

She glided her gaze downward, studying the narrowness of his hips, the way his jeans cupped his butt. "Anyone?"

"Any noncommittal woman," he clarified.

"Like the women you're used to dating."

"Yeah, I suppose any of them would do." He finally

spun around, facing her once again. "Unless you're volunteering."

The breath in her lungs rushed out. She felt instantly light-headed, stupidly swoony. To keep herself steady, she clutched the rim of the sink. "I'm not a party girl."

"I know."

"Then why did you say that?"

"Because I wanted you ever since I saw you again."

Her misbehaving libido wanted him, too. But she knew it wouldn't solve anything. "We can't. We shouldn't. It wouldn't do either of us any good."

"I know," he said for the second time.

But he'd still brought it up. Was it his way of clearing the air, of getting the feeling out of his system? She wasn't about to ask him if it helped.

It wasn't helping her. If anything, it reminded her of how inexperienced she was.

"I've only ever had one lover," she said, confirming how truly different she was from him. "I haven't been with anyone except for my ex."

He frowned. "You must have been married for a long time."

"No, actually, it was a short marriage. It only lasted about three months. But I knew him a long time. I met him when I was nineteen, and we dated on and off for eleven years."

Tanner's frown deepened, lines crinkling at the corners of his eyes. "So, is it safe to assume that you didn't wait until you were married to be together? Otherwise, your timeline doesn't make a whole lot of sense."

"That's a safe assumption." She moved away from the sink, busying herself with the leftovers. The way Tanner was studying her made her feel like a traitorous virgin under a microscope, the same silly girl who'd fussed about the importance of a wedding night. "It happened about a year into our relationship."

"When you were twenty?"

"Yes, and I married him when I was thirty."

"And now you've been divorced for four years?"

"That's right." The math wasn't complicated, but the story was, and it seemed obvious that Tanner was thinking the same thing.

"If you dated on and off for eleven years, then why weren't you with anyone during the off times?"

"If I gave myself to another man, I was concerned that it would diminish what I'd built with him." She scrunched up her face, cursing her loyalty. "He was with other women when we weren't together, though."

"He sounds like a prince." He made a sarcastic sound. "Why do guys like that always get the best girls?"

Was that supposed to make her feel better? She rounded on him, clutching the cheese platter in front of her. "I seem to recall you breaking up with me, not the other way around."

He backed down. "You're right. I'm sorry. I guess I'm just feeling betrayed because he got to have you, and I didn't."

"He doesn't get to have me anymore."

"Apparently no one does."

"I don't have affairs. That isn't something I'm comfortable doing."

"If you ever decide you want to be wild and free, I'd be glad to accommodate you."

She set the platter down. "Don't push your luck."

He had the gall to grin. "Can't blame a guy for trying."

"Really? That how you're going to play this?" She fired a little square of cheddar at his chest.

It hit him in the vicinity of his heart.

But he didn't seem to notice the implication. Would it have been smarter to aim for his fly? Whatever the case, he laughed and looked for something to pelt her with.

He found the leftover kebabs, and she widened her eyes. If he speared one of those at her, he could do some serious damage.

"Ha!" he said, wielding it like Zorro. "I just scared you, didn't I?"

He scared her in lots of ways, even when he was just kidding around. "Truce?" She held out her empty hands, ending the food fight before it went too far.

"Okay, truce." He removed the tofu and vegetables from the skewers and put them in a ziplock bag. Then he asked, "Why was your marriage so short? Three months is nothing, especially after how long you'd known him."

Now she wished that she'd let him stab her with a kebab. Or a knife. Or a sword. Anything to keep her from having to answer the question. She didn't want to tell him about the baby she'd lost. Not only did it hurt too much to say it out loud, to reveal the absolute truth about her marriage, they'd already had too many painful baby discussions.

She kept her response vague. "He just said it was a mistake we made." A baby they hadn't meant to conceive, a marriage that shouldn't have happened. "We had one of those quickie Vegas ceremonies."

"With just the two of you?"

"No. Our parents were there. He's close to his family. He wouldn't have left them out."

"Who is he, anyway? What's his name?"

"Vince McCall. He's a fashion photographer. I met him when I first started modeling. In fact, he was the photographer my mom hired to shoot my portfolio pictures. He was already fairly well established by then."

"I'll bet your mom didn't blame him for the divorce."

She wished that Tanner wasn't so astute. Or so inquisitive. "No, she didn't." The fault had been Candy's for getting pregnant and insisting on keeping the baby. "She admired him for trying to boost my career. To her that was more important than me marrying him." Or having a baby, she thought. "Mom was fine with me being Vince's lover. She thought that was more glamorous than me being his wife."

A muscle ticked in Tanner's jaw. "She forbade me from going into your bedroom, but she encouraged you to be with him."

"I was of age when I was with him."

"You should change your name back to Sorensen. You shouldn't be Candy McCall anymore."

She considered his suggestion, wondering why she hadn't done it before now. Was it because McCall would have been her baby's surname? "Maybe I will. Maybe after escrow closes, I'll have time to deal with it."

"That's a good idea. Start fresh. Start new."

"You'll be starting over, too."

"Don't I know it." He smoothed his hair. A few short strands had fallen onto his forehead. "I still need to get raging drunk and have tons of sex."

"So this conversation is back to where it started?"

His grin returned, slower, sexier. "Are you sure you don't want to tie one on with me? I've got a big bottle of tequila back at my apartment, just waiting for me to crack it open."

She wished that she was the type who could handle something so cavalier. That she could toss back some shots, smile like a siren and lick salt off his naked torso. "Maybe in another life."

"Like in heaven?"

Or in hell, she thought as they finished cleaning the kitchen, without another word about it.

Tanner went home and spent the rest of the evening scrolling through the contacts on his phone, looking for a willing woman. Tonight, tomorrow night or any night that she was available. It didn't matter, as long as she was happy to oblige.

But he kept moving past the same names and numbers, without stopping on any of them.

Every time he came to the *C*'s and saw Candy's contact information, he hesitated, tempted to call her.

And say what? That he couldn't stop thinking about her?

He was becoming the king of longing, of wanting what he couldn't have. Funny, how history repeated itself. He didn't have a shot with her when they were young, and he didn't have one now, either. But at least he'd gotten to touch her when they were kids, to kiss and dance.

He wasn't getting anything now, except friendship.

Good, kind friendship, he thought. The bond between them was becoming genuine again, and for that he felt blessed.

But that didn't ease his hunger.

He scrolled through his numbers again, focusing on his original agenda. Mindless sex and a sleep-until-noon hangover. He had the right to party, to blow off some steam before he buckled down to take care of Ivy. Besides, he could always fantasize that his bedmate was Candy.

Really? a voice in the back of his mind said. *You'd use another woman in place of her?*

He told his conscience to shut the hell up, but it didn't listen. The voice remained, warning him to forget the drunken date. But that didn't stop him from obsessing about Candy.

Maybe she would sext with him. That wouldn't be like a real affair.

Yes, it would, the voice said. The electronic stuff counted. He couldn't use it as an excuse to lure her into something dirty.

Tanner snarled his frustration, wanting to bop himself in the gut. Or someplace where it would hurt.

So how about a friendly call, just to hear her voice, just to see what she was doing? There was nothing illicit about that.

He pulled up her contact info and let his phone dial the number. It rang in his ear. If she didn't answer, he was going to feel mighty stupid for sitting here battling with himself.

"Hello?" Her voice came on the line. She sounded surprised, but she obviously knew it was him. His name would have appeared on her screen.

"Hey," he said, trying to sound casual.

"What's going on, Tanner? What's up?"

"Nothing. I was just bored and thought I'd call to see how the rest of your night was going."

"I was just getting ready to soak in the tub."

That wasn't what he needed to hear. Envisioning her

naked and wet was the worst image she could've presented. "You must be exhausted."

"I am. It was a long day."

"You worked hard on the barbecue." But that wasn't what was on his mind, especially now that she'd mentioned soaking in the tub. This friendly call was torturing the crap out of him. He decided to come clean. "Truthfully, I didn't ring you up because I was bored. I was looking for someone to sleep with, but called you instead."

Her breath hitched, low, shaky. "I have no idea what I'm supposed to say to that."

"Nothing, I guess. But just so I don't seem like a total dog, I want you to know that I haven't played around in a long time."

"How long?" She sounded suspicious, as if she didn't trust his concept of time.

"I don't know the exact date. I'm not even sure who my last partner was. But I do know that it's been around five or six months."

"Not remembering who you were with isn't helping your cause."

"I still sound like a dog?"

"Yep."

"At least I'm telling you about it. I'm not close enough to the women I sleep with to confide in them about Ivy, and ever since I agreed to become her guardian, I've been too stressed out to be with anyone. Sex has been the last thing on my mind."

"But then you ran into me and your desire came back?"

"Pretty much, yeah."

"I don't know whether to be flattered or confused by that."

He didn't know, either. All he knew was how she affected him. The heat. The wanting. The restraint. The uncharacteristic envy over her ex.

"Who else knows about the baby besides me and Eric and Dana?" she asked. "Have you told anyone that you work with? Or any of your other friends?"

"Not yet. Every time I think I'm ready to say it, I can't seem to find the words."

"Oh, Tanner." She heaved a sigh. "You can't hide it forever."

"I know. I'm working up the courage."

"Not saying it isn't going to make it any less real."

"I just don't want anyone judging my sister or gossiping about what she did. Nor do I want to have to bring the baby around for everyone to see her. I need to get used to her first."

"You will. After she arrives, it'll get easier."

He sure as hell hoped so. "Do you want to hang out with me on your next day off? Just as friends," he clarified. He'd already convinced himself to stop pursuing her.

"Sure. That sounds nice. Where should we go? What should we do?"

"We can go bowling," he said and made her laugh. "Or you can come by and I'll give you a tour of my stables."

"Actually, I'd like to see where you work and live."

"Okay. Then it's a…" He almost said *date*. But he didn't want to use that word. "Just let me know what day works for you, and I'll arrange my schedule to fit yours. We can go riding, too, if you'd like."

"I haven't been on a horse since you and I were together. But I'd like to give it a go, as long as you have a horse that'll accommodate a novice like me."

"We definitely do. We have horses for every level of rider."

After they agreed on a day and time, she asked, "We're talking about going out on trail, right? Not doing fancy, jumpy things in an arena?"

"Yes, I'm talking about a quiet Western ride. Did you honestly think that I would put you in a situation you weren't ready for?"

"You were trying to get me into bed."

"I'm not trying anymore."

A beat of silence passed. Then another. He wasn't sure what to do, other than to sit there, alone on his bed, with the phone pressed to his ear.

Finally she said, "I'm going to go soak in the tub now. But I'll see you next week." She paused, then added, "Take care."

"You, too." He ended the call and tried not to think about her, the girl he couldn't have, stripping off her clothes for the bath.

Chapter Six

What a morning, Candy thought. She was meeting Tanner at his stables today, and she labored over what to wear. She'd already donned jeans and a simple shirt. Her clothes were easy enough. But the shoes were giving her trouble.

She had a pair of old cowboy boots stuffed in the back of her closet. She'd bought them at a thrift store years ago because she thought they were fun and funky, but she'd never worn them.

She found the boots and slanted them a suspicious glance. They were ridiculously fancy, made of soft brown leather and embroidered with pink roses.

Flowers, she thought, on her feet.

Would she look stupid for wearing them to this outing? Oh, come on, she told herself, they were a logical choice, considering they were designed for riding. She was making too much of this.

She slipped them on over her skinny jeans and checked her reflection in the mirror. They didn't look half-bad. The fun and funky factor was still there.

Trying to keep things natural, or as natural as a woman in flashy footwear could be, she did a light application of makeup and flat-ironed her hair.

But something wasn't quite right. It was her top, she decided. It was too plain for the boots. She needed a nicer balance between the two. So she went back to her closet and pulled out a pale pink cotton blouse with gathered sleeves.

It worked much better. She looked sleek yet sassy. She made a goofy face in the mirror. The next boots she bought were going to be less noticeable.

What next boots? She wouldn't be making a habit of this. One little visit to Tanner's place of business didn't warrant another pair of boots.

Candy brewed a cup of mint tea and fixed steel-cut oatmeal for breakfast, buying a little time to calm her nerves. The telephone conversation she'd had with Tanner—the bit about her being the object of his desire—weighed on her mind. The scariest part was that she'd been going through the same thing, with him bringing her dormant libido back to life. He'd been celibate for about five or six months, and she'd been sex-free for four years. The odds weren't in her favor.

But it didn't matter because they weren't going to act on those feelings. She'd made it clear that she wasn't wired for an affair, and he'd extended an invitation to be friends and nothing more.

So why did she have butterflies in her stomach? Friends shouldn't make friends nervous.

She stirred her tea and watched the liquid swirl.

Eventually he would give up the fight and take another woman to his bed. Wouldn't he?

Of course he would. But it was none of her business what Tanner did or who he hooked up with.

Then why did it leave her with an uneasy feeling in the pit of her divorced heart? At some point, Candy was going to meet the man of her dreams.

She was going to get married again and have children and be blissfully happy. Or so she kept telling herself. At the moment, all she felt was lonely.

She frowned at her oatmeal. She'd only taken a few bites. The butterflies in her stomach were interfering with her appetite.

She gave up on breakfast and sat on the front porch. Soon, it would be time to leave, but for now she gazed out at her freshly mowed lawn. The gardeners had just left, leaving the scent of cut grass in the air. It should have been comforting, but it wasn't. That supposedly refreshing smell was caused by chemicals in the grass trying to heal itself from the injury that had just been inflicted.

Of all things for Candy to think about today.

Finally, she quit stressing and climbed into her car. Her lawn would survive the trauma. It would continue to grow, lush and green, as it always did.

Twenty minutes later, after a minor bout with surface-street traffic, she arrived at her destination.

It was a beautifully maintained facility, offering a big breezeway barn, indoor and outdoor arenas, round pens, cross-tie areas, wash racks and everything else a horse enthusiast could want.

Even on a weekday morning, there was plenty of activity, with people grooming, exercising and riding the animals they boarded. The stable that housed the rental horses was on the other side of the property, near the trails that led to the park, and she suspected it was just as nice.

She headed to Tanner's office, where they'd agreed to meet. It wasn't the main office, where the rest of the managerial staff worked. It was a separate two-story building, surrounded by a redwood fence and located near a copse of trees.

She went inside and found him sitting behind an L-shaped desk, talking on the phone. He looked up and smiled, but she hung back, letting him finish his conversation. It sounded as if he was booking rentals for one of the studios. He'd told her that his company provided horses for the movie industry. He'd come a long way from the stable hand he'd once been.

He completed the call and rose to greet her. "Wow. Look at you." He scanned her from head to toe, running his gaze, those powerful eyes, up and down. "And check out the boots."

"I got them from a thrift store."

"Pink roses." His smile was rife with approval. "What do they mean?"

"I don't know. I hadn't really thought about it." She'd been too nervous about seeing him to consult the Victorian dictionary about her feet. "I bought these before I started reading up on floriography."

"Then let's find out, shall we?" He sat on the edge of his desk and spun his laptop around.

While he got online, she checked him out. He looked damned fine in his Western gear. His clothes consisted of various hues of timeworn denim. He had a penchant for black, she noticed. His boots were black, like the

English ones, only these were scuffed instead of shiny. He even had a black hat sitting on a stack of paperwork. His belt was a moonlit shade of midnight, too, with little silver skulls on it. It made him seem wild, like a cowboy biker who knew just how to straddle a horse. Or ride a woman, she thought.

"Thankfulness, admiration and happiness," he said.

She blinked. "I'm sorry. What?"

"That's what pink roses mean."

She cleared the heat from her mind. "I gave them to myself, so that's a good sign."

"I like your top, too. I wondered if you still wore that color, and you do. I used to call you cotton candy when you wore pink."

She hoped that he didn't call her that today. She didn't want to be compared to something that would melt in his mouth.

"So, where should we start?" he asked. "Do you want to see my apartment first?"

Now she wished that she'd never expressed an interest in wanting to see where he lived. But she wasn't going to wuss out. "Sure. Let's start there."

He escorted her to an indoor stairwell, located at the end of a short hallway. At the top of the landing was a door that led to his apartment.

They went inside, and he said, "This is it."

Candy glanced around. The open plan showcased polished oak floors, a strongly furnished living room, a barely used kitchen and a rustic dining area with a solid-wood table and a scrolled-iron chandelier. He didn't have a lot of knickknacks, but the artwork on the walls was Western, with some Native artifacts scattered in between.

She shifted her attention to the portable bar in the corner. Was that where the unopened bottle of tequila was being stored? The get-drunk-and-have-sex invitation?

"Your place is really nice," she said, turning away from the bar. It was definitely a bachelor pad, with a masculine vibe.

"I cleaned up since I knew you were coming." He shot her a slightly crooked smile. "I even made my bed."

As curious as she was to see where he slept, she didn't want to think about his bed or get anywhere near it.

A heartbeat later, they were still standing in the same safe spot. Thankfully, he didn't give her a tour of his room. Making his bed, she assumed, was just a formality.

But that didn't stop her from wondering how long it would take for him to resume his sex life and return to the wild-and-free women he was used to dating.

"What are you going to do with the extra beds in your house?" he asked.

"What?"

"In the guestrooms? Are you going to keep both of them in storage? Because I was thinking, if you want to sell the entire outfit that's in the first guestroom, I'll buy it. I'll need to furnish a room for the nanny, and everything you already have in there would work out nicely if you're not going to keep it."

"Sure. I can sell it to you. I was going to put a number of things on Craigslist and that bedroom set was one of them."

"Before you place the ad, let me know, and I'll take as much stuff off your hands as I can. Since I'll be holding on to this apartment, I'm going to have to get furniture for the new house, too."

"No problem. We can work that out."

"Have you started packing already?"

"Yes, but I still have a ways to go." To keep herself busy, she moved to the other side of the living room and glanced out a big picture window that overlooked his property. "You have a great view of your operation." She could even see a glimpse of the hills in the background.

"It's been my home for a long time." He joined her where she stood. "I bought it eight years ago."

"I had no idea that you'd been here that long."

He turned to face her. "I couldn't have done it without the money my mom loaned me."

"I couldn't have bought my house without the inheritance I got from my grandparents. They would be mortified if they knew that I couldn't afford to keep it."

"I nearly lost this place," he reminded her.

"But you saved it." He obviously had a better business head than she did. She was impressed with what he'd accomplished. "Your mom must have been proud."

"She was. My brother and I got our love of horses from her. She inspired both of us to pursue careers in this industry." Tanner glanced out the window again. "The money she loaned me was part of what she'd gotten in the divorce settlement. At least my dad didn't try to screw her out of what he owed her. But I guess it was easier for him to just pay it and get on with his life."

"Rather than let it drag out in court?"

He nodded. "The financial part was easy. It was the emotional stuff that was a mess."

The financial aspect of Candy's divorce had been

easy, too. But there weren't any money ties between her and Vince. They hadn't even lived together before they'd gotten married.

She thought about the situation she was in now. "I can't believe I'm in transition again."

"Don't worry. You're going to be okay."

"And so are you. With Ivy, I mean."

He smiled, a bit too softly. "We're always telling each other that everything will be all right."

"So it seems." She wanted to wrap her arms around him and indulge herself in a body-warming hug. But they'd yet to embrace, and this wasn't the time to start, not after the friends-only agreement they'd made.

In most cases, hugging didn't lead to sex, but she knew better than to risk it, especially when the mystery of his bedroom was just around the bend.

"I chose a magical horse for you to ride," he said, drawing her into a new conversation.

"Magical?"

"A white horse. All she needs is a sparkly gold horn in the center of her head to look like a unicorn."

She sighed in remembrance, sweeping herself back in time. "Unicorns were my girlish obsession."

"I know. You used to say that you wanted to ride one, like in those fantasy movies we used to watch."

She thought about the stress associated with her youth, the perfection that had been expected of her. "Sometimes I used to imagine disappearing into a world of make-believe and never coming back."

"Now's your chance. For a few hours, anyway."

"What's the mare's name?"

"Enchanted."

"That's beautiful, Tanner." A white horse, a faux

unicorn, called Enchanted. That was as close to magic as a grown-up girl like Candy could get.

Tanner rode beside Candy on the trail, thinking how magnificent she looked paired up with Enchanted. Technically, the horse was a few-spot leopard Appaloosa that didn't actually have any spots. Although she had some pale gold hairs around her knees, elbows and hocks, her overall appearance was white. Tanner thought she was a stunning creature, with an equally wonderful temperament, a prized lesson horse with the ability to adapt to the skill of any rider.

And then there was the other female, in her pink top and rose-embroidered boots. Spun sugar in the form of a woman, he thought. She kept glancing over and smiling, as if this really was a magical adventure.

But maybe that was exactly what it was. Maybe at any given moment, Enchanted would sprout a gilded horn and lead them into a realm where nothing was real.

And everything was idyllic.

Tanner's mount, a no-nonsense gelding, snorted, bringing Tanner back to reality. Until Enchanted tossed her pretty head again.

He said, "Did you know that according to medieval legends, unicorns can't be tamed, except by the innocence of a maiden?"

Candy adjusted herself in the saddle, shifting her gorgeously shaped rump. "I don't know anything about the habits of unicorns. I just liked the idea that they could exist." She glanced at him from the corner of her eye. "How do you know about those old legends?"

"I got curious and did an internet search on it this

morning before you came over. It's funny how the innocent thing keeps presenting itself."

"Only because you've become aware of it. It's like when someone mentions a certain type of car, and then you see one everywhere you go."

He reined his horse to a stop. "So I should expect to see maidens everywhere I go?" He looked both ways. "Honestly, I don't see any. Do you?"

She stopped, too, playing along. "Do they even exist anymore? I think they might be extinct."

"Actually, come to think of it, I do see one." He slid his gaze over her. "Yes, I definitely do."

She continued the banter. "Is that so?"

He smiled, winked, kept the joke going. "Yep, and she smells good, too. But that's part of a maiden's innocent allure."

"Really?"

He couldn't resist his answer. He even leaned toward her, pretending to take a whiff. "They're sweet, just like…candy."

"You're the worst." But she laughed anyway.

He liked making her laugh. It was certainly better than making her sad, like he'd done when he'd broken up with her those seventeen-some-odd years ago.

Clearing the past from his thoughts, he called attention to their surroundings. "How great is this trail? I love it out here."

"It's amazing."

Tanner nodded. They were in a wide-open space with an abundance of greenery, as well as a spectacular view of the chaparral-covered terrain, the park's urban wilderness, in the canyon below. "This land is my home away from home."

"I can see why."

He glanced at the flowers blanketing the nearby landscape. "What are those?"

"What are what?"

"Those bright yellow flowers."

"They look like primrose to me."

"What do they mean?"

"I don't know. I haven't memorized all of the symbolism yet. I'm still at the stage of reading about it."

He removed his phone from his pocket. "I'll check." He got online and typed in the *meaning of primrose* as he'd done earlier with the pink roses. "Okay, here we go. It says, 'I can't live without you.'"

She raised her eyebrows. "You can't?"

He smiled, glad that she was treating it lightly. "Oh, wait. There's another meaning, too. Guess what it is?"

"I have no idea."

"Innocence."

Candy clucked her tongue. "It is not."

"It is, too." He handed her his phone. "See?"

"Oh, my goodness. That's just too weird."

"Yeah." He grinned and took his phone back. "But considering how strict the moral codes were back then, they probably gave tons of flowers that meaning."

"Obviously."

"Are you sure you still want to plant flowerbeds with old-fashioned messages in them?"

"I'm sure. But I'm going to be careful what combinations I choose."

"No innocent plants next to dangerous ones?"

"It's better to keep them separated."

In spite of her comment, he was tempted to jump off his horse and pick a bouquet for her. But he didn't. He wasn't courting her. Nor was he supposed to be luring her into an affair.

Nonetheless he said, "So if a man gives a woman a primrose, with the intention of combining the meanings, is he saying 'I can't live without your innocence'?"

"That's as good as any interpretation."

"Yeah, I guess it is." They continued their ride, but they couldn't escape the primrose. It grew aggressively on the sides of the road. Dangerous in its innocence, Tanner thought.

Much like his friendship with Candy.

Chapter Seven

Candy was up to her eyeballs in boxes, but she didn't mind. Escrow was scheduled to close in two days, and she appreciated that Dana was helping her with the final packing.

Unfortunately Candy's mom, the mighty Jo Sorensen, had bulldozed her way in, insisting on helping, too. The three of them were in the kitchen, wrapping glassware and dishes.

Her mom was busy doing what she did best—complaining. "It's such a shame that you have to sell this house. And to think who's buying it. I never cared for that boy's family. There was just something about them that didn't sit well with me. So doesn't it figure that his sister is in prison?"

Candy had made the mistake of telling her mom about Meagan and the baby. And now she understood why Tanner had been so cautious about sharing that information. Of course, no one could react any worse than her mom.

Even Dana was being deliberately quiet, trying to avoid being pulled into the conversation. Candy didn't have that luxury. The discussion was being directed at her.

"Tanner was handsome, though," Mom said, actually tossing in something nice. "Tall and dark, with those wild gray eyes. Does he still look good?"

"Yes, but he has a good heart, too," Candy replied.

"Does he?" Mom didn't sound convinced. "Why? Because he's going to take care of his sister's child? If he was smart, he would've let social services handle it. That baby would be better off in foster care."

"How can you say that? He's Ivy's uncle."

"What does he know about raising a little girl? You said he's been a bachelor all this time."

"At least he's going to try. Besides, in his culture, being an uncle is equivalent to being a father."

"If his sister hadn't committed a crime, he wouldn't be stuck in that situation to begin with. I'll bet she's going to be a terrible mother when she gets out."

Really? Candy thought. This from the woman who'd made her childhood miserable?

Mom studied a set of salt and pepper shakers shaped like frogs. "Why are you keeping all of this junk?"

Candy blew out her breath. "Because they're cute. And because *The Frog Prince* was my favorite fairy tale."

"Fairy tales are foolish."

But forcing her daughter to become a beauty queen wasn't? When she was a child, wearing those dreaded tiaras, she used to fantasize about meeting a frog who was a cursed prince, certain that he would understand that she'd been cursed, too.

"So Tanner is back in your life," Mom said suddenly. "Please tell me that you're not going to start dating him again."

Candy tried not to flinch. She wasn't about to admit that she was still attracted to him or how tenderly their non-romance was playing out. "We're just friends."

"And he owns a horse facility?"

"Yes. His operation is quite fancy. They even rent horses to the studios."

"Who knew he would grow up to be so successful? I certainly didn't." Mom sounded impressed but jealous, too.

She'd always been obsessed with the entertainment industry, with actors and models and singers. Candy assumed that was why her mom had pushed her so hard to be recognized as one of the beautiful people.

But Mom was an enigma. For someone who was obsessed with how other people looked, she hardly ever fixed herself up. She'd always worn her short brown hair in a matronly style, making her appear older than she was. She rarely fussed with makeup, either. Nor did she wear flattering clothes or take care of her figure.

She worked as a secretary, and most of what she'd earned had been used for Candy's dance lessons, beauty coaches and ball gowns. They'd even lived with Candy's grandparents to make those things more attainable. But now Mom had her own tidy little house, with no one to micromanage or boss around.

She wrapped the frogs and reached for another set. "How many salt and pepper shakers do you need?"

Candy replied, "As many as I want. I collect them."

"I think they're adorable." Dana finally piped up, using a cheery voice. "Vintage collections are fun."

"It's a waste of money." Mom sent Candy a sour look. "Is it any wonder you can't afford to keep your house?"

The doorbell rang, and Candy thanked the heavens for the interruption. She didn't care who was there or what they were selling, as long as it gave her an escape.

Except that Dana beat her to it. Her friend said, "I'll get it," and zoomed out of the kitchen.

Dang it. Dana owed her for that.

Soon the blonde returned with Tanner in tow. "Look who it is."

Yes, look. There he was. Tall and dark with those wild gray eyes. Mom stopped packing and stepped out from behind her box. Candy's pulse leaped, like one of the ceramic frogs come to life.

"Speak of the devil," Mom said, gauging his hot-as-hell appearance. "We were just talking about you."

He flashed a lethal smile, as if he was conducting business with an old enemy. "Then my ears must have been burning." He paused. "So, how are you, Jo?"

She thinned her lips. "I'd be better if my daughter didn't have to sell her house."

He glanced at Candy and then stood up for her the way he had when they were teenagers. "She's going to land on her feet."

Mom arched her body, reaching around to rub the swell of her back. "I hear you're doing well. That you have yourself a fancy horse facility."

"You'll have to come by and see it."

As if, Candy thought.

Mom said, "I'm not an equestrian, but I always thought dressage was classy."

"We give dressage lessons. Maybe you can give it a try."

Mom waved away his comment, rolling her eyes and shaking her head. "I've got other things going on."

Tanner didn't drop it so easily. "You're welcome to come there anytime." When she snorted like one of his horses, he added, "It's a standing offer."

"Then I suppose we'll have to see," Mom told him.

Candy wasn't sure what to make of their conversation. But at least it was over and no blood had been shed. She motioned to Tanner, and they went onto the porch.

"I came by to see how you were doing," he said. "But I didn't expect to see your mom."

"I didn't expect for her to be here, either." She sat on the top step and dusted her hands on her jeans. "Would you really give her dressage lessons?"

"If she truly wanted to learn, I would." He sat beside her. "But apparently her opinion of me hasn't changed."

"She's just ticked because you can afford to buy my house. She thinks it's foolish for you to help raise Ivy, too. But I know you're going to prove her wrong."

"Thanks for coming to my defense. By the way, I ordered a three-piece nursery set today. A crib, a dresser and a changing table. I haven't scheduled the delivery date yet. I'll do that as soon as I move in."

Candy would be moving on the day escrow closed, but the house wouldn't be vacant. She was leaving behind the furniture he'd purchased from her. She was also letting him borrow some other pieces, rather than put them in storage. She trusted that he wouldn't damage anything, and it made her feel better to know that the house would look much the same. "I'm glad you found something for the baby's room that you like."

"It's white. That seemed to be the most common color. I chose the crib because of how well rated it is. Don't forget that you offered to go shopping with me for the rest of the stuff."

"I haven't forgotten. Once you're settled and the nursery is put together, we can shop. I'll get online and download a checklist of things you'll need."

"Your help means a lot to me, especially now that the due date is getting closer."

"I'm glad to do it. I cohosted Dana's baby shower. It was at her house. She got all sorts of great gifts." She shot him a silly grin. "Maybe we should have a shower for you."

"Perish the thought." He kicked his booted feet out in front of him. "I wish Meagan was getting to experience those sorts of things, though."

"I know. I understand." His sister was missing out on all the joy of having a baby. "But she's lucky that she has you."

"I started the nanny search. I've been working with an agency. Hopefully, I'll have someone lined up soon. The nannies who are newborn-care specialists book fast, so they told me not to wait too long."

"You'll have someone in no time."

"That's the plan. How's your packing? Are you almost done?"

"Yes. But I wish I didn't have to go back into the house and face my mom. I'd just as soon run away today."

"I'd let you sneak off with me, but I suspect she would hunt you down."

"No doubt." And running away with him wasn't a

good idea, no matter how glorious it sounded. Regardless, she asked, "If we did take off, where would we go?"

"Anywhere you want." He placed his hand on her knee, then quickly removed it, as if he'd done something wrong.

But it didn't matter. His fingertips had already sent sexy shock waves through her system. She assumed that he felt it, too. Or why else would he have jerked his hand away?

"I better get going," he said, in a sudden hurry. "I have appointments this afternoon."

"Yes, I'm sure you're busy." She wasn't going to try to keep him, not with the way they were making each other feel.

"I'll be in touch," he said as they stood up.

Being in touch wasn't the same as actually touching. Or kissing. Or dancing. Or having sex, she thought, as she watched him walk away.

But even after he left and she returned to the kitchen, she couldn't get him off her mind. Candy was trapped in the temptation that was Tanner.

Two weeks passed, with Candy adjusting to the changes in her mixed-up life. She still hadn't found another part-time job, but she continued to look, hoping for the best. And now, of course, she was staying with Eric and Dana.

As for Tanner, he was coming by today so they could shop for baby goods. Her attraction to him was still as strong as ever, but she tried not to dwell on it.

When he arrived, she took a deep breath and greeted him with a smile.

"Where is everyone?" he asked upon entering the living room.

"Eric and Dana took Jude to the park. They took Yogi with them, too." Though Candy thoroughly appreciated being here—it was a nice place, with Dana's creative touch—she missed the house she'd sold to Tanner.

He extended the canvas bag that was in his hand. "I brought you some lemons, like I promised I would."

"Thank you." She clutched the bag, feeling as if she were clutching a piece of the house that was no longer hers. "I'll make meringue cookies with them."

"I'll bet it's a healthy recipe."

"It is." She headed for the kitchen.

Tanner followed her, and while she arranged the fruit in a bowl, he asked, "Will you save some of the cookies for me?"

"Of course. I'll make extras just for you."

He glanced out the window that overlooked the backyard, then leaned against the counter. "I hired a nanny. She can start whenever I need her, so she'll be moving in next Tuesday. That will give her a week to get acclimated before the due date, so even if Ivy arrives a little early, the nanny will be there. She's just what I'd hoped to find—older, highly experienced, bright and friendly. She raised a big family of her own. She's from England, and she has the coolest accent."

Candy teased him, "You hired Mary Poppins?"

He laughed. "I've never seen that movie, but I suppose I did. Her name isn't Mary, though. It's Libby."

"Libby Poppins?"

"Libby Jones."

"I'm looking forward to meeting her."

"You'll like her, for sure. And I'm so relieved. Of

everyone I interviewed, she's the only one who fit all of my criteria. She's going to take care of the baby, but she's also going to teach me how to do everything. She was really sweet about Meagan, too. Some of the other nannies were uncomfortable about the prison aspect and having to bring the baby there, but Libby is fine with it. She's going to accompany me whenever I visit Meagan."

"She sounds like a gem."

"She is. Do you want to visit Meagan sometime, too?"

"Yes, I would love to see your sister." She was touched that he was bringing her into the fold. "I have no idea what's expected of me, though. Do I have to get approved first?"

He nodded. "There's a visitor's questionnaire that Meagan will have to send you with her signature. After you fill it out and sign it, you return it to the prison, and they run a background check on you."

"I'm okay with that." She didn't have anything to hide.

"Once you're approved, you'll have to follow their rules, like how to dress, what items you're allowed to bring and the types of activities they permit. Visiting hours are Saturdays and Sundays from eight to three."

"I'd be glad to go whenever I'm available."

"It will be nice to have you there." He frowned. "If you can call something like that nice."

Deciding it was time to change the subject, she said, "Let me show you Jude's room before we go shopping. Eric and Dana decorated it in a zoo-animals theme. Eric painted the animals on the walls. It was his way of protecting Jude with Native totems. He even wrote out the spiritual meanings next to them."

She took him down the hall, and they entered the room. She stood back and watched Tanner check everything out. He seemed mesmerized by the animals: the Trickster Coyote, the Mother Earth Turtle, the Gentle Deer, the Introspective Bear, the Magic Raven.

"The Wolf is Dana's favorite because of the teacher symbolism," Candy said.

"Because Eric is a teacher?"

"Yes, and Butterfly is Eric's favorite because it represents transformation, and he says it's Dana's spirit guide."

"Which is Jude's favorite?"

"He seems to like them all. He's got stuffed animals everywhere, too, as you can see. It's a happy room."

"I want Ivy's nursery to be happy, too. I wonder if we should create a theme. If it was up to me, I'd use horses or ponies or something, but Meagan isn't into horses the way I am, so it doesn't seem fair to choose a theme that my sister won't connect with."

"What do you think Meagan would choose?"

"I have no idea. But she would probably just tell me to do whatever feels right. She's cautious about interjecting too many of her thoughts and feelings about what she considers my house." He reached for a toy monkey and played with its floppy arms. "Maybe we can do a magic-castle theme since Meagan named Ivy after a princess. Besides, my sister loves that kind of stuff. She still talks about the enchanted stories our mom used to read to her."

"That's a wonderful idea. Castles and clouds and winged horses."

He grinned. "You just came up with a sneaky way

of slipping some horses into it. We might as well add a few unicorns, too."

Her pulse fluttered. "I'm good with that."

"This is going to be fun."

Too fun, she thought. Candy steadied her breath, reminding herself that this wasn't her child. That no matter how close she got to the situation, Ivy didn't belong to her.

"What's wrong?" he asked suddenly.

"Nothing."

"You're frowning."

"I was?" She made a lame excuse. "I must have gotten sidetracked with the way you're tugging on that poor monkey's arms."

He patted the toy's head, as if to apologize to it, and put it back where he got it. "What do you think of incorporating falling stars into it?"

"For making wishes?"

"Yes, but also because Falling Star is a Cheyenne folklore hero, and that might be a nice way of bringing my culture into it, like Eric did with his."

Curious about the folklore, she asked, "Why is Falling Star a hero?"

"He fell from the sky when he was in his mother's womb, then grew up to save his people from a terrible monster." Tanner stood beside Jude's crib. "His mother didn't survive the fall. She broke into pieces because she wasn't originally from the sky, but Falling Star was made of star material, so he couldn't break."

Candy wished her baby would have been made of star material. "What happened to him after he hit the ground?"

"A meadowlark picked him up and put him in her

nest with her babies. She and the father meadowlark raised him with their young until Falling Star was old enough to go off on his own."

She imagined her little one living with a family of meadowlarks. Her lost baby. The miscarriage she still hadn't told Tanner about.

He said, "We should definitely try to find some items with stars on them. Having them around might help make Ivy strong."

"Then we'll do our best to find as many as we can." She wanted his niece to be strong. Unbroken, she thought.

"Did you download the checklist from the Net?"

"It's in my purse."

He moved away from the crib. "Are you ready to go?"

She nodded, and they left the house. She sat beside him in his truck, thinking about the broken baby she'd lost.

Once they arrived at the store, Candy got herself together. She removed the checklist and said, "We should probably focus on the essentials first. Then we can search for the other stuff."

"How many essentials are there?"

She handed him the two-page list. "Take a look."

He widened his eyes. "All of this for one little baby?"

"And that's just for starters. There's going to be a lot more as she gets older."

"Damn. Are you sure you don't want to just crack open a bottle of tequila and get drunk with me?"

"Tanner." She didn't need the sexual implication that went with his joke. The heat. The hunger. The fantasy of sleeping with him. "I'm being serious."

"So am I. Look at this frigging list. Hmm. I think

some of it might be a problem. Nursing bras? A breast pump?"

"Okay, funny guy. Just pay attention to things you will need."

He scanned the list again. "I hadn't even thought about a diaper pail or a hamper, let alone a cradle or a rocking chair."

"Well, now you're thinking about it."

"My head is going to explode."

"Quit being so melodramatic and grab a cart."

"A cart? We're going to need a forklift."

They grabbed two carts, one for each of them to push.

"How am I supposed to fit a cradle or a rocking chair in here?" he asked.

There he went, kidding around again. Obviously, some things would have to be delivered.

She said, "I think we should look for a daybed for the nursery, too. That way, the nanny can sleep in there while she's adjusting to Ivy's feeding schedule. Most parents keep their newborns close to them at first."

"That's a great idea. I'd prefer knowing someone is with Ivy as much as possible. I can crash in there on the nanny's days off."

Once they started shopping, they worked well as a team. Choosing the car seat and the stroller took quite a bit of time. So did analyzing the monitors that were available. Candy suggested the one Dana and Eric had used for the first year of Jude's life since it had a SIDS-type safety feature.

As they continued to browse, Tanner marveled over the little things, like how tiny the clothes were. The linens fascinated him, too. They found a quilt with a pink-

and-gold castle on it, along with an assortment of crib sheets and receiving blankets embellished with stars. He grabbed stacks of those, certain they'd hit the jackpot. He even found a mobile that played "Twinkle Twinkle Little Star," which became the most prized possession of all. The rest of the theme they'd chosen, the winged horses and unicorns, came in the form of lamps, stuffed animals and switch-plate covers.

They returned to his house—her old house—and unloaded his truck, dumping everything in the nursery.

He ordered pizza, and they ate while she helped him organize. By the time they were done, the room glittered in sweet infant magic.

Candy could have stayed there forever, pretending that this was still her house and that Ivy was her baby. But it wasn't, and no amount of dreaming was going to change that.

Now she wondered if she should spend less time with Tanner, if it would be healthier for her to distance herself from him and Ivy and Meagan, including the visitations she'd agreed to attend.

Only in order to do that, she would have to tell him about her miscarriage and explain why this wasn't good for her.

But at the moment, immersed in the nursery they'd just designed, she couldn't summon the strength to do it.

Chapter Eight

Candy spent the following week trying to decide what to do about her dilemma with Tanner. Luckily, she had Dana as a sounding board. They gathered in the living room, with Jude playing on the floor nearby. Surrounded by plastic alphabet blocks, he banged them together, gasping with excitement from the noise they made. He was the epitome of a California kid in his toddler muscle shirt and beach-inspired board shorts. Candy envisioned him when he was older, with his naturally tanned complexion and bad-boy dimples, skateboarding and surfing and making girls sigh.

He smacked the blocks together again, with even more gusto, and she wished that she had his enthusiasm for life. At the moment, she was suffering from mental exhaustion.

"Things should be easier than they are," she said to Dana.

"I'm sorry that being around Tanner is becoming difficult for you. It seemed to be coming along so nicely. A good, solid friendship."

"Aside from the attraction we've been fighting, it has been going well. But now I'm afraid that I'm going to get overly attached to him, especially once the baby comes."

"Maybe you won't see him that much. He'll be busy with Ivy. Besides, the nanny will be there. It's not like it's going to be you and Tanner and a newborn in a homey situation."

"You're right. I'm probably making more of it than it is."

"I wonder if you should just give in." Dana talked above the noise Jude was making. "And let it happen."

"What do you mean? Let what happen?"

Her friend grinned, her blue eyes sparkling. "Get drunk and have sex with him."

"That's not funny." Candy grabbed one of Jude's stray blocks and threw it at Dana, bouncing it off her bodacious boobs.

The toddler looked up and laughed. His mama did, too. Candy envied the joy between them.

Dana looked as impish as her son. She was dressed in a tie-dyed top with faded food stains, courtesy of Jude, along with holey jeans decorated with embroidered appliqués. Her hair was banded into what Eric commonly referred to as a Gidget ponytail. She also wore a fake flower, typical of her bohemian style, clipped at her ear.

"I want it all," Candy said. "To have what you have." A husband, a baby, true happiness.

"I know, sweetie. And someday you will have it. But for now, you just need to take it one day at a time."

Eric came down the hall and entered the living room. He'd gotten home from work a little while ago, and now he was ready to kick back with the family.

Candy tried not to feel like an intruder.

Jude exclaimed, "Dada!" and ran over to his father, stumbling at his feet.

Eric reached down and scooped up his son, wrapping one strong arm around him. Yogi appeared next. She'd been down the hall, too.

When Jude saw her, he gave her the same excited welcome. "Dog!"

Yogi went over to him and sniffed his bare foot, and he giggled, her wet nose tickling him. Even Candy's pet was becoming part of the household.

There were two cats that lived here, too, but they barely reacted to the dog, other than a few hisses when she'd first arrived. Since then, they'd milled around in their usual way, going in and out of the back door.

Everyone was having a fine time, except for Candy. She hated that she was feeling sorry for herself. But she wasn't a naturally upbeat person, not like Dana. She wished that she was, though.

Candy glanced over at Eric. He wasn't like Dana, either. He was more like Candy, cautious by nature. He'd shut himself off from the world after his first wife died. He'd taken care of his daughter, but he hadn't dated until Dana had come along, seven years after he'd become a widower. But now here he was, married to the second love of his life and experiencing the wonderment of fatherhood again.

Candy reached for another of Jude's blocks, turning it in her hand. Would she ever get to experience the wonderment of motherhood? With each lonely day that streamed by, it was getting tougher and tougher to convince herself that her dream would come true.

"Someone's phone is ringing," Eric said. "I think it's yours, Candy. It sounds like it's coming from your room."

"Thanks." She dashed past him, grateful for an excuse to give him and Dana and their son time alone as a family. She was even skipping out on Yogi, who remained with Jude.

The room she was staying in had belonged to Kaley, Eric's grown daughter, when she was a teenager. Borrowing her former room made Candy feel a bit like a teen, too. Along with her renewed association with Tanner, of course. These days, her old boyfriend factored into everything.

Just as she jumped across the bed and nabbed her cell phone on the nightstand, it stopped ringing. She checked the notifications and scrunched up her face. It was a missed call from Tanner. Should she return it? Or avoid him for now?

Within seconds, the phone rang again, with Tanner's name popping up on the screen. Clearly, he was impatient to reach her. Or he was calling back to leave a message.

Avoiding him didn't make sense. She just needed to suck it up and stop worrying about her self-centered feelings. She spent all kinds of time with Jude. It shouldn't be any different with Ivy. A baby was a baby. Besides, as Dana said, there was a nanny involved. Candy's role wasn't as important as it seemed.

Before the call went to voice mail, she answered it with a nice and normal "Hello?"

"Oh, thank God," he said. "I'm so freaked out, Candy. I don't know what to do."

"Why? What's wrong?"

"Libby can't take the job. She had to go back to England for a family emergency. Her father had a stroke, and she's going to stay there and take care of him. Before she left, she assured me that the agency would provide another nanny, but I can't handle being around a stranger. I trusted Libby. She's who I hired, and now she's gone."

"Don't panic, Tanner. You've got about a week before Ivy is due. Maybe even a little longer, if she's late. There has to be someone—"

"No, you don't understand. Ivy was born yesterday, but they didn't call me until today."

Her pulse nearly jumped straight out of her skin. "She's here already? Is she okay? Is Meagan all right? Have you seen them?"

"They're both fine. I'm not allowed to visit Meagan for security reasons, but I talked to her on the phone. They're keeping Ivy in her room, so at least she's getting a little time with her daughter. Ivy weighs seven pounds two ounces and is as healthy as a newborn should be."

"Oh, thank goodness."

"Yes, but tomorrow morning Meagan will be transported back to prison, and I'm supposed to pick up the baby at the hospital." His voice went rough. "But I can't do it. I can't go there by myself. Will you go with me?"

"Yes, of course." She couldn't refuse to help him, especially when he was in such a fix. "But you're going to have to talk to someone at the agency to see what nannies are available to take Libby's place. Maybe you can use someone in the interim, then keep interviewing until you find a permanent one who suits your needs."

"I was hoping that you'd take the job."

"Temporarily?"

"No. For good."

She went into shocked silence, needing a moment to grasp his words. Finally she said, "You want me to move into your house and take care of Ivy?" To be there day and night, with him and the baby? "I'm not a professional nanny. I can't do something like that." She couldn't put herself in the middle of his life, not when she was already worried about becoming too attached.

"You'd be a great nanny. I know you would."

He didn't know the half of it. He didn't know about her lost child or the emotional impact this would have on her. But she couldn't bring herself to say it. She just sat there, clutching the phone.

He asked, "You still need a second job, don't you?"

"Yes." She was down to two part-time days at the studio. Her job situation had gotten worse, not better. "But this isn't the answer."

"Think about how it will benefit you. It's a good wage, with free room and board. Plus, you can have whatever days off you need to teach your classes. I'll fill in when you're not around. I'll do whatever I have to do to make it worth your while."

She argued her case, pointing out the obvious. "I don't see how you and I are going to manage living together."

"You can live in the guesthouse after it's remodeled. We can make a nursery out of the second bedroom, and we can shift Ivy back and forth between us. So you'll only be living with me until the remodel is done."

"Why are you so adamant about me being her nanny?"

"Because I trust you, more than Libby, more than anyone. You're like family to me. You know everything there is to know about me and mine. You were there when Ella died, and I want you to be there to help me keep Ivy strong and healthy."

Trapped within the painful beauty of his words, she drew her knees up to her chest. How was she supposed to say no to him? Yet, if she said yes, her role in his life would become frighteningly important.

"I'll never find another nanny who will be as right for this job as you are, Candy. Remember the primrose at the park? The 'I can't live without you' message? That's how I feel right now. Ivy and I can't live without you. We need for you to help us."

More beautiful words. More pain. He'd just tied her up with a primrose bow. But could she become the nanny? Could she risk getting attached to him and Ivy in that way?

"Please," he implored her.

Candy prepared to make an excuse. But heaven help her, she couldn't cut the tie.

Trying to keep herself centered, to sound as professional as possible, she said, "I'll take the job, and I'll do the very best I can to take care of Ivy. But I want you to follow through on getting the guesthouse remodeled. It's important for us to live separately as soon as we can." At least that would keep her and Tanner from getting too close, from their lives intermingling any more than necessary.

"That's not a problem." His breaths rushed into the phone. "Thank you so much. I don't know what I would have done if you'd refused. When I found out that Ivy had already been born, I felt like I was having a heart attack. I still feel like I am. My heart hasn't quit pounding."

"We'll get through this together, I promise. But for now you need to relax. Just call me in the morning and tell me what time you're going to the hospital, and I'll be ready. Not just to go with you, but with my bags packed to move in."

"Do you think you could come over tonight instead? I'd feel better knowing you were already here. You can get settled into your room and do whatever you need to do. I think it would make tomorrow less stressful."

Once again, she couldn't say no. And what difference did an extra evening make if she was already going to be staying there? "Give me a few hours, okay?"

"Sure. You can bring Yogi, too, of course. She's part of the deal. Oh, and when you get here, can we go to the market? I have no idea what type of food to have on hand for you. I need groceries, too. Mostly I eat in restaurants or grab stuff on the go. But with Ivy being around, I'll be staying home more than I did before."

"That's fine. We can go shopping. I'll see you in a while. Oh, and will you call the hospital and find out what type of formula they're feeding Ivy? I'm sure they'll give you some to take home, but it probably won't be enough to last more than a few days. We can get more at the market."

"Good thinking. I'll call them right now."

He thanked her once more, and they hung up. Earlier she'd been wondering if she should avoid Tanner, and now she was becoming Ivy's nanny.

She returned to the living room to tell Dana and Eric

what was going on, and they offered to help in any way they could.

Dana also questioned Candy privately about her decision. "Are you sure you can handle this?" her friend asked.

"I hope so," she replied, even if she was feeling the fear, the full-blown reality, the pulse-jarring impact, of what she'd just agreed to do.

Candy appeared on Tanner's doorstep with Yogi on a leash and a pile of luggage. He'd never been so glad to see anyone. But he felt like a ghost, too, as if he were floating through the events of the day. He'd tried to be prepared for Ivy, but she'd arrived at the same time that Libby had quit.

And then there was Candy, his beautiful friend, coming along to save the day. He couldn't thank her enough.

Initially, she wasn't the sort of nanny he'd envisioned. He hadn't intended to have the object of his desire around. She was right about them living separately as soon as the guesthouse was redone. Being in the same house with her was going to be a major distraction. But his niece's well-being came first, overriding any other concerns he had.

Clearing his thoughts, he helped Candy with her bags, and she removed the dog's leash. Yogi wandered around, checking out the changes that had been made to her old home, then curled up in the living room beside the fireplace, embracing a familiar spot.

Tanner and Candy barely talked now that she was there. He lingered in the background, letting her settle in.

She unpacked, hanging up her clothes in the guestroom and putting away toiletries in the bathroom she would be using. He was impressed with how organized she was.

Once she completed the process, she asked, "Are you ready to go to the market?"

"Sure." He reached into his pocket and handed her a scrap of paper with the name of the formula on it.

She added it to a list that she'd already made. Definitely organized. In spite of her determination to get everything done, he could tell that she still had a lot on her mind. But why wouldn't she? He'd just roped her into becoming an on-the-spot nanny.

They took his truck to the store. Once they went inside, he walked beside her while she pushed the cart.

Quite a few heads turned in their direction, but they got attention whenever they went out together. He figured it was because she was so pretty. But he stood out, too, with his height and whatnot. Noticeable as they were, he doubted that anyone would guess the nature of their relationship. They probably looked like a couple to the outside world.

"I've never done this before," he said as she stocked up on the formula.

"Done what?"

"Gone grocery shopping with a woman."

"Not even your mom or sister?"

"They don't count."

She added diapers to the cart, lots and lots of them. "They're still women."

"You know what I mean." He grabbed a ton of baby wipes and tossed them in, helping her stockpile the infant goods. "Do you think that when we go out with Ivy she'll be mistaken as our daughter? That other people will refer to her as ours?"

Candy hesitated to respond. Then, after waiting until another patron walked by, she said, "If they make that assumption, we can just tell them the truth."

"That my sister is in prison and it's her kid? That I'm the legal guardian, and you're a girl I used to date, who I begged to help me?" If he wasn't so stressed out, he might've laughed at the ridiculousness of it. "That will make them glad they struck up a conversation with us."

"Jeez, Tanner." She shook her head. "I wasn't implying that we give them that much detail."

"So we should keep it simple? Like I'm the baby's uncle and you're the hot nanny I want to get naked with?"

She made a face at him. "That isn't funny."

"Sorry. I won't make cracks like that again."

"Yes, you will. It's in your nature."

"Okay, then I'll try not to. But you have to admit that if we tell people the truth they'll probably assume that we're having a fling. The chemistry between us isn't hard to miss."

She fussed with the items in the cart, rearranging them. "There's nothing we can do about that."

"It's just that we'll be wrongly perceived, either way. Mistaken for the baby's parents or stereotyped as lovers. But you're right, it doesn't matter." He needed to keep his priorities straight, regardless of the obstacles they had to confront.

He owed Candy big-time, and he meant every word he'd said to her on the phone. She was the person he trusted most in the world—the nanny he and Ivy couldn't live without.

* * *

Candy fixed a late dinner. She made a chicken casserole for Tanner, and roasted vegetables for herself. She also prepared a mixed-green salad and conjured up a batch of sweet-potato fries for them to share. For dessert, she served cinnamon-spiced applesauce.

Neither of them had eaten that evening, and now that there was food in the house, she was able to cook a hearty meal. Plus it helped her stay busy. Otherwise, she would be fidgeting.

They sat across from each other at her old dining table. She hadn't sold it to him, but it was one of the pieces that she was letting him borrow.

He dug into the casserole and said, "You seem sort of wifely tonight."

She could do little more than blink. After their discussion at the market, that wasn't what she needed to hear.

"Cooking seems wifely to me," he explained. "And cleaning and taking care of kids. All of the old-school stuff."

She relaxed and reached for her fork. At least his opinion was generic, and not necessarily specific to her. Curious to know more, she asked, "So what makes a man seem husbandly, in your opinion?"

"I'm not sure. I had a poor role model in that regard. My dad was a bad partner to my mom."

"I know about bad husbands, too." That was something she couldn't deny.

He swigged his water. "Has Vince ever been here?"

She wasn't sure what he meant. "Been where?"

He gestured to their surroundings. "To this house. Did he ever come over after you were divorced?"

"No." There was no reason for them to visit each other after it was over. "I haven't seen him since I moved out of his loft."

"That's where he lives? In a loft?"

"Yes, in the Fashion District, where his studio is."

"Is that where he shot your first portfolio pictures?"

"Yes." It was the place where everything had happened, she thought. Where she'd lost her virginity, where he spent the night with other women during the times they'd broken up, where their baby was later conceived, where the miscarriage had occurred. "But there's no point in us talking about him. Vince is no longer part of my life."

Tanner gazed across the table at her, deeply, intensely, almost if he were trying to see into her soul. Then he said, "I owe you my life for what you're doing for me."

Her heart went shaky. She didn't want him looking at her like that. "You don't need to take your gratitude that far."

"But I'd be falling apart if you weren't here with me."

"Comforting you with a warm meal?"

"It definitely helps. And for the record, I wasn't trying to trivialize women being wives. It's just that cooking and cleaning and taking care of kids is what I saw my mom do."

She thought about the falling-out he'd had with his father. "Do you think your dad knows that Meagan is in prison?"

"I doubt it. None of us have spoken to him in years, and he hasn't tried to contact any of us, either."

After a moment of silence, she contemplated her

own family dynamics. Then she said, "I wish my mom wasn't so closemouthed about my father."

He leaned forward in his seat. "What do you know about him?"

"Just that his name was Dan Sorensen, and he was an orphan who grew up in a group home in the Midwest. He came to California when he was in his twenties and made his living as a roofer."

"How did he die?"

"It was a roofing accident, but I don't know the details." She gazed at her half-eaten food, immersed in thoughts of a dad she couldn't remember. She looked up and asked, "How did your mom pass? You never said how it happened."

"She had heart failure. But it had been broken long before that. First from losing Ella and then from my dad leaving her." He stirred his applesauce, his spoon clanking against the bowl. "I don't ever want to be responsible for breaking a woman's heart. Making a commitment to someone else is too much pressure."

"Is that why you ended it with me when we were kids?"

He nodded. "I just couldn't handle getting so close, especially not at that age."

"I understand that you were young and scared. But it was still a bleak decision for a seventeen-year-old boy to make."

"My baby sister had just died, and my parents were gearing up for a divorce. Bleak was what I knew. But later, I got used to being a bachelor, without having to worry about any ties."

"And now you're going to be Ivy's legal guardian, with me involved in her care."

"My old girlfriend. The nanny who cooks and cleans and epitomizes my perception of a wife. God really did a number on me, didn't he?"

She smiled, though it was twisted. "Your punishment for breaking up with the best girlfriend you ever had."

"More like the only girlfriend I ever really had. The ones that came before you didn't last beyond a few weeks. I spent six months with you. That was epic for me."

"The entire duration of Ella's young life."

"I never really thought of it that way. But you're right. That's the time frame we were together. I started going out with you soon after she was born and ended it soon after she was gone."

When the memory between them got too heavy, she said, "Maybe we should talk about something else."

"Like what?"

"Ivy," she said. The baby who had just been born. "Did the rocking chair and cradle arrive for her nursery?"

"They were delivered yesterday."

She adjusted her napkin. "That was good timing."

"No kidding. The daybed came, too. Is that where you're going to sleep after we pick her up?"

"If I'm going to be getting up every few hours to feed her, I'd rather be in the same room with her, at least until I know her routine. But I'm fine with keeping my belongings in the guest room."

"Until the guesthouse is remodeled and you move in there?"

She resumed eating. "Yes, until then."

"I told my staff about Ivy. Not that she was born yet.

I haven't had time to do that. But last week I came clean about why I bought a house and what was going on."

"Was it as difficult as you thought it would be?"

"Not really. Everyone was really nice about it. They wished me all kinds of luck. None of them know about Ella, though. They aren't familiar with my past." He frowned. "Sorry. I can't seem to stop myself from mentioning her."

Refusing to fault him, she softly said, "If it makes you feel better, you can say whatever you want about Ella."

"Your compassion makes me feel better."

"I'm glad it helps." At least he was honest about his feelings. Candy was still keeping a painful secret from him. The loss of her child, she thought, the little one who'd fallen from her womb.

He said, "I don't think I'll be able to sleep tonight. I'll probably stay up and start reading those baby books I bought."

She'd studied child development during her pregnancy. She'd been so excited about having a baby that she'd absorbed everything there was to know. And now, as a nanny, she would be putting that knowledge to use, along with what she'd learned from being around Jude.

He spoke again. "I think we've got good start. Don't you?"

Perplexed, she asked, "What do you mean?"

"With you and me." He motioned back and forth, between them. "With this arrangement."

She hesitated, thinking about the secret she was keeping. Then, forcing herself to act normal, she replied, "We've covered a lot of ground, particularly with how fast it unfolded." But there was still more ground that hadn't been covered.

The ache she couldn't bear to reveal.

She glanced across the table at him. By now, both of them were finished eating. "I'm getting tired. I think I'm going to load the dishwasher and get ready for bed."

"I can clean up. It's the least I can do."

"Thanks. That would be nice." She appreciated that it took her out of wife mode, too. She didn't want to feel like his rendition of a bride every time she did domestic chores around him. Preparing to leave him with the dishes, she stood and pushed in her chair. "I'll see you in the morning."

"You, too." He carried their plates into the kitchen.

She watched him, then ventured down the hall, hoping that she could shut down her troubled mind and sleep.

Chapter Nine

Candy tossed and turned for hours, with a zillion things still running rampant through her head. But mostly, she obsessed over one subject.

The child she'd lost. The secret she was keeping from Tanner. Not admitting the truth to him, especially now that she'd agreed to become Ivy's nanny, made her feel like a terrible friend, a liar and a cheat who was pretending not to have baby issues.

She reached over and turned on the light, squinting from the glare. Should she give up the fight and tell him? And if she did, was this a bad time to broach the subject on the night before Ivy would be coming home?

When would be a good time? After his niece was here, tucked away in her nursery? What difference did it make when she said it, as long as she told him?

So why wait? *Do it now. Get it done and over with.*

She went to the closet and slipped on her robe. She couldn't go to his room in her skimpy pajamas, her tank top and itty-bitty shorts, without a cover-up.

She checked her reflection in the mirror, making sure she didn't look the slightest bit sexy. No tousled hair, no come-hither gaps in her robe.

Truthfully, she probably shouldn't be going to his room at all. But at this point, she just wanted to say what she had to say, even though she knew he was in bed. She'd heard him shut down the house not more than thirty minutes ago. By now, he would be reading up on baby care, or so she assumed. If he'd ditched the books and turned out the light, she wouldn't bother him.

After one last mirror check, she padded down the hall. She noticed the light shining under his door, so she went ahead with her plan.

She knocked and called out, "Tanner. It's Candy."

She winced after making the announcement. Who else would be rapping at his door at 11:00 p.m.?

"Come in," he called back.

Suddenly, she stalled. What if he got the wrong impression and thought she was there to seduce him, even with her proper appearance? Oh, sure. As if she would trick him like that.

Forging ahead, she turned the knob, convincing herself, once again, that she was doing the right thing. Backing out wasn't an option.

Upon entering the room, she saw him reclining in bed, propped against a bunch of pillows, with an e-reader in his hands. She'd envisioned a pile of paperbacks strewn around him.

The room was rugged and masculine, in shades of brown with strong accents of black, far different than how she'd decorated when she'd slept there. His bed wasn't her old bed. It wasn't a piece of furniture that she'd offered to let him borrow. That would have been way too weird.

"What's going on?" he asked. He sounded concerned, as if she was going to be the bearer of bad news.

It was probably the expression on her face. Or maybe it was the way she was clasping the front of her robe, white-knuckling the heavy cotton fabric.

She replied, "There's something I need to tell you."

"I'm listening."

"May I sit down?"

"Of course." He patted the space next to him.

She'd been thinking more along the lines of a chair, but there weren't any. How dumb of her not to have noticed before now. What hadn't gone unnoticed was his sleeping attire. His chest was bare, and he wore a pair of boxer shorts, the elastic waistband partially obscured by the covers draped around his hips.

Candy sat on the corner of the bed, warning herself not to react, even if she'd never seen him in his underwear before.

He turned off the e-reader and placed it on the nightstand, a blast of worry dashing into his eyes. "You aren't changing your mind, are you?"

"About taking the job? Goodness, no. I wouldn't do that to you." She wouldn't bail on him when he needed her. "I just…" She hesitated, preparing to say what was on her mind.

"You just what? Come on, Candy, what's going on?"

All right, she thought. *Here goes.* "I want to tell you about something that happened to me. About the baby I lost, so you know where my emotions are coming from."

He started, his big, broad shoulders jerking backward. "You lost a child?"

"It was a miscarriage. It's also the reason my marriage only lasted three months. Vince married me because I got pregnant, and after the baby was gone, he didn't see the point of staying together anymore."

"I'm so sorry." He pushed the pillows out from behind him and moved to the center of bed, closer to the edge where she was.

As the covers fell away from his half-naked body, she clutched the front of her robe again. "Vince admitted that he wasn't in love with me. He was glad when I lost the baby because being married to me was making him feel trapped."

"He sounds like my father. Cripes, Candy. What did you see in him?"

"I was delusional, I guess. Because, really, I should have known better. If he'd loved me, he would have wanted to marry me years ago instead of keeping me on a string with our on-again, off-again relationship."

"Did you convince yourself that it was going to work after you got pregnant?"

She nodded. "Yes, but I didn't conceive on purpose. I thought we were being careful, but the birth control we were using failed." She quickly added, "Even though it wasn't planned, I was secretly thrilled when it happened. All I've ever wanted was to be a wife and mother."

He watched her with empathy, making her far too aware of the baby they would be sharing. It made her think about Meagan, too, being forced to let her child go.

Candy expelled the air in her lungs. "Vince was upset when I got pregnant, but he never suggested that I terminate. He just asked me what I was going to do. And when I told him that I was going to keep it, he offered to marry me, for the sake of the child. It seemed so honorable at the time, so old-fashioned. But he came from a proper family. It was how he was raised."

Tanner frowned. "I guess we're all a product of our environment in one way or another."

"It was a huge factor in why he proposed. He knew his parents would have pressured him to do it anyway. And they liked me. They thought I was a nice girl."

"You are a nice girl." He spoke softly, his voice comfortingly quiet. "I can't imagine anyone not liking you."

She glanced away for a second, needing to compose herself. "Being liked by them was wonderful, but not being loved by their son was a killer. And the loss of our child, of my baby, left me feeling more alone than I'd ever been."

"Why didn't you tell me any of this before? Why didn't you mention the baby?"

"For a lot of reasons. But mainly because I couldn't bear to say it. It's been four years, but it still affects me. Helping you prepare for Ivy made me long for what I'd lost. And it was becoming so difficult, so hard to handle, I was considering spending less time with you. On the day we decorated the nursery, I had to keep reminding myself that Ivy wasn't my baby."

Tanner went unbearably silent. During those clock-ticking minutes, Candy stared into space, wishing he would say something to resume the conversation.

Finally, he did. He said, "It's not right."

She shifted her gaze back to him. "What isn't?"

"That I roped you into becoming Ivy's nanny. How

are you going to hold that baby in your arms, struggling with those kinds of feelings?"

"That's why I'm telling you about it. Because I don't want to feel that way. I want to heal from losing my child and not fantasize that Ivy belongs to me."

"When I brought that sort of thing up at the market, about how people are going to perceive us as Ivy's parents, it must have struck a painful chord for you."

"It did. But now that it's out in the open, I can work on it. But you have to help. You have to treat me like the nanny and not your surrogate wife."

He made a terribly troubled face. "I haven't been doing that. Besides, what do I know about having a wife? I've never even been in a committed relationship. All I said earlier was that you seemed like the wifely type. That isn't the same as behaving as if we're married."

"I guess it's just me, gearing up for living in my old house with a man I'm attracted to, along with the baby we'll be caring for."

"Being attracted to each other doesn't make us pseudo spouses. Nor does us taking care of Ivy."

"You're completely right. It doesn't."

He shifted on the bed, stirring the mattress, the weight of his body creating a strange sort of intimacy. She could almost imagine him drawing her into his arms, in spite of the warning she'd just given him.

Then suddenly he asked, "Do you still love Vince?"

The question brought her up short, especially in the wake of her thoughts, but she answered it. "No. Not anymore."

"I'm glad you aren't still carrying that around with

you. My mom continued to love my dad, even after he hurt her."

"I did that for a while, too. It's hard to let someone go, even when you know you should."

"At least you got past your feelings for him." He looked her straight in the eye, with a devilish smile. "Now all you need to do is keep it in perspective and not fantasize about being married to me."

"Oh, please." She couldn't help but laugh, which was what he wanted, obviously. "You'd be a lousy husband."

"That's just my point. It would be a stupid fantasy." He leaned forward and poked her in the rib. "But just in case, I'll act like a dork, so you'll get turned off by me."

She poked him back. "You already do that now."

"Then I guess you're doomed by my charms."

She smiled at his silliness, but she spoke honestly, too. "Truthfully, I was worried about getting attached to you. But I can work on that now that we've had this conversation. There's nothing left to hide. It's all out in the open."

"Is it?" he asked.

"Yes," she assured him. Yet in spite of her assurance, they stared at each other as if the air between them had gone soft and sweet.

Without breaking eye contact, he said, "I'm still nervous about picking up the baby tomorrow. But it helps that you're going to be there."

She breathed in the honeyed air, the heat, the proximity of him. But before she did something stupid, like fantasize about him being her husband, she said, "Will you be able to talk to Meagan again? Before they transport her back to prison?"

"Yes. They're going to allow her to call in the morning. She doesn't have a phone in her room, so it has to be arranged."

"Do you think I would be able to talk to her then, too?"

"I don't see why not. Since you're here with me, I can hand you the phone so you can say hi. I'll be sure to tell her that you're the nanny."

"I wonder how she'll feel about that."

"I think she'll be glad that it's you instead of someone she doesn't know."

"Even though you sang Libby's praises?"

"I've been singing your praises, too, about what a good friend you've become. My sister is happy that we've been hanging out and that I bought your house. She already mailed the application for you to visit her in prison. She sent it late last week when I first mentioned it to her. I had her mail it here because I didn't know Eric and Dana's address. I was going to give it to you when it arrived, but now you're living here, so that worked in our favor."

"I'll fill it out and send it back as soon as it gets here." She knew how important it was.

"Thank you again for being so supportive of me and Meagan and Ivy."

"You're welcome." Because she was feeling much too warm, much too connected to him, she got up to leave. "I should go back to bed. I really do need to get some sleep."

"I should sleep, too. I wasn't getting much reading done, anyway. It was tough to concentrate."

"You'll get up to speed."

"I'm going to try." He lowered his gaze. "'Night, Candy."

She glanced down and realized that her robe had opened, revealing a glimpse of her pajamas. The skimpy ensemble she'd been trying to hide from him.

Rather than scramble to close it, she pretended that it didn't matter, then braved her way to the door and said good-night, too.

Tanner buckled the infant seat into his truck. He and Candy would be leaving soon to pick up Ivy, and already it had been a gut-wrenching morning. They'd spoken to Meagan on the phone, and he'd fought a flood of pain, hearing his sister's sad and lonely voice.

"Is this right?" he asked, not having a clue as to what he was doing.

She came forward to check the straps. "Yes."

"Are you sure?"

"I'm positive. Jude's first one was similar to this. I know how it works."

He didn't like feeling so anxious, so inadequate, so frustrated over a device he would be using every time he took Ivy somewhere. "When we take her home today, will you make sure she's buckled into it the way she's supposed to be? I don't want her to slip out."

She put the diaper bag in the truck and turned to face him. "I won't let anything happen to her, and neither will you."

He looked into the warmth of her eyes. She was a hell of a friend. Yet to keep the moment in check, he took a deliberate step back. If she were the type of friend who was sharing his bed, who was comfortable with those sorts of benefits, he would tug her into his arms for a comfort-between-lovers kiss. But especially after everything that had been said last night, he was even more cautious about crossing those boundaries.

"Ready?" he asked.

She got in the passenger side. "As ready as I'll ever be."

Following suit, he climbed behind the wheel. But he didn't start the engine. He needed a quick breather before getting on the road.

"Are you all right?" she asked.

"I just wish the hospital was closer." Ivy was born at a medical center near the correctional institution that had become his sister's dreaded home, which was over eighty miles away. "I should be used to going in that direction by now, from all of those visits to Meagan. But it still feels like a long trek, particularly today." He frowned, giving himself a moment's pause. "Do you know what Meagan said to me on the phone? That she didn't want me to bring the baby to see her right away. She's worried about having Ivy exposed to so many people, especially in a prison environment. She asked me to wait at least a month, when the baby's immune system will be stronger."

"I can understand how she feels. But it's going to be difficult for her, too, being away from her daughter for so long." Candy heaved a sad sigh. "She asked me to tell Ivy that her mama loves her, to say it every day, the way Meagan would if she could."

He finally started the vehicle and backed out of the driveway. "I hope Ivy helps you."

Out of what seemed like habit, Candy wrapped an arm around her middle. "What do you mean?"

"To get over your loss." He did his best to smile.

"It would be great to think of Ivy as a superhero baby, coming along to save your heart."

She smiled, as well. "That's sweet, Tanner. I like that."

He was glad that he'd lifted her mood, right along with his own. "We'll have to buy Ivy a cape."

"And fly her around the house."

"Yeah, I can just see her, riding high in our arms until she can run and play and pretend to take flight on her own. She can pretend to fly at night, too, among the stars."

"When you told me the Falling Star story, I wished that my baby would have been made of star material."

Shiny and unbreakable, he thought. When she'd come to his room last night and relayed her story to him, he'd wanted to protect her, to hold her. But he'd been careful not to do anything that would create more emotion between them. "Was Vince with you when you miscarried?"

"No." She clutched her middle again, pressing against the seat belt. "He was away on location, on a shoot. I was by myself. Bleeding and cramping and crying. It was the most traumatic day of my life. I called an ambulance for myself, but by the time they got there, I knew it was too late. That my little one was already gone."

"I'm sorry that you had to go through that alone. If I could have been there for you, I would have."

She studied his profile. He could feel her looking at him, analyzing him. Then she said, "Maybe you wouldn't be such a lousy husband after all."

He jerked his head toward her, nearly giving himself whiplash. "Please tell me you're joking."

"I am." She laughed a little. "Sort of."

"No sort of, missy. I would suck at it. Maybe not in the way Vince was a crummy husband. Or my dad. But I'd be a failure just the same."

"At least you're a kindhearted person."

"That still doesn't make me husband material."

She shifted in her seat. "I know. Besides, I'm going to find the right man someday. Even Dana keeps telling me I will."

He headed toward the freeway on-ramp, fighting a twinge of envy, envisioning her with a nameless, faceless groom waiting for her at a flower-draped altar. Flowers with personalized messages, he thought, chosen just for the wedding.

Annoyed by the scene in his mind, he said, "I understand how important it is for you to find Mr. Right. But whatever you do, don't leave me and Ivy behind so you can run off with him."

She rolled her eyes. "I'm not leaving anyone."

Selfish as it was, he couldn't bear to do this without her. "Promise?"

"Yes, I promise." She turned on the radio, as if she was trying to make the drive less intense. She kept switching stations, trying to find something she liked.

Neither of them had downloaded music for the trip or packed any CDs. They'd had too much else on their minds, so now they were at the mercy of whatever was playing on the airwaves. He hoped she didn't latch on to a song with a twisted marriage theme, like Beyoncé kicking men's asses for not putting a ring on it. Or Elvis lamenting about people having suspicious minds. Or George Strait's exes living in Texas.

"How about this?" Candy asked.

"The Backstreet Boys?" He all but gaped at her. That

was even worse than the songs he'd envisioned. "What part of me says boy-band fan?"

"Oh, come on, where's your sense of nostalgia? They're totally from our era."

"I never listened to them."

"You did, too. We even danced to this at your prom."

"We did not." It was true, they had. But he was pretending that he didn't remember gyrating to it.

"You're just pissed because I had a crush on Nick Carter." She fluttered and swooned. "He was the bomb."

"Are you kidding? That dude's got nothing on me." To prove his point, he started singing along with the song, acting like the dork he claimed he could be, mimicking every word, every inflection, every "wooo" in the background.

She burst out laughing, but he kept crooning about rocking his body. Or her body. Or anybody's body. He sang the sexy parts louder than necessary, making her laugh harder.

Candy joined in, being a dork, too. She bobbed in her seat. She knew all of the dance moves from the old video. As embarrassing as it was, so did he. He tossed in a few of them, without going overboard. He didn't want to cause an accident, cruising down the freeway having a bit of idiotic fun with the beautiful new nanny.

En route to picking up a superhero baby.

Chapter Ten

The fun and games ended when Tanner and Candy arrived at the hospital. He wasn't feeling lighthearted anymore. His nerves had kicked into high gear.

They entered the big, sterile building, becoming instantly immersed in its sky-blue decor, blinding-white walls and antiseptic smell. He wanted to dash back outside, but he couldn't run off like a kid on his first day of school.

"This is it," he said to Candy, fighting to keep himself grounded. "The moment of truth."

"You've come this far. You can do the rest of it."

"What if the baby doesn't like me?"

"She's going to be crazy about you, Tanner."

"It's such a heavy responsibility." It would be his place to nurture Ivy, to teach her, to feed her, to clothe her, to give her everything a little girl should have. And even after Meagan was released from prison, he would still be deeply involved in the baby's welfare, as well as his sister's rehabilitation. "I know this is a hell of a time to say this, but what if I really did bite off more than I can chew?"

"You shouldn't be thinking that way, not now. Besides, I'm here to help you through it."

He passed the main reception desk and headed toward the directory to see what floor the maternity ward was on, his boots making more noise that he would've liked. She walked beside him, her soft-soled footsteps quiet.

He considered the time frame of their agreement. "How long will you be available to help me?"

"For as long as you need me."

"Your job as the nanny will end when Meagan comes home."

"That's two years away."

"I know, but after that, I wonder what's going to happen."

"What do you mean?"

He studied her beneath the fluorescent lights. Even saturated in its glare, she looked soft and pretty. "With us. With the way we're building our friendship."

She stood beside him at the directory. "You're still not making sense."

"It's just that our friendship might fade away. Not because I'll want it to, but because you'll be married with kids of your own and living your authentic life. And that probably isn't going to include you hanging out with me." To him, it seemed like a no-brainer, even if it troubled him to think about it.

A frown creased her brow. "What's your authentic life? Being an uncommitted bachelor?"

"It's worked for me so far." At this point, it was the only world he knew. "But if Meagan never gets her act together, I won't able to go back to who I used to be. I'll be spending the rest of my days trying to save my convict sister."

"You need to give her more credit than that. And maybe you aren't meant to be the same guy as before. People are supposed to change."

"Not if those changes don't feel right." Already he was turning into someone he didn't recognize, worrying about staying friends with Candy and missing her before she was even gone. He shouldn't be relying on her as heavily as he was, but he knew damned well he couldn't face this challenge without her. "Will you take the baby when they first give her to us? I don't think I can handle carrying her out of this place."

"Yes, of course. I totally want to hold her. And once you're able to relax, so will you."

She was the most encouraging person he knew, and even though she'd lost a child, she was putting herself out there for him and Ivy. "You're going to be a great mom someday."

"Thank you." She smiled. "That means a lot to me."

Once again, he wished that he could kiss her. Today of all days, he needed the taste of a woman's lips. But not just any woman's. Hers, he thought. The nanny. He didn't doubt that Ivy was going to feel safe in her arms.

He couldn't lean in and kiss her, not without breaking their platonic agreement. But by the same token, he couldn't continue to stand there, in a public place, hungry for something that wasn't going to happen.

"We should go," he said.

She nodded, and they proceeded to the elevator.

The maternity ward was on the third floor, and the ride up was crowded. No one spoke, but it was just a bunch of strangers packed together, with Lord knew what on their minds.

The door opened on their floor, and he and Candy exited the elevator. As they headed for the nurses' station, they walked down a corridor with a mural on the wall, depicting a cartoonish tree decorated with pink and blue booties hanging from its leafy branches.

They reached the station desk, and Tanner got the ball rolling, explaining who he and Candy were. The head nurse came forward to help them. She was an older redhead, friendly and efficient, dressed in colorful scrubs. She shook their hands and introduced herself as Joanne, which was also on her name tag.

He wondered if she was one of the staff who'd been nice to Meagan. He wished that his sister was still here and that he could walk into her room with a cluster of "It's a Girl!" balloons. But that wasn't how this arrangement worked. By now, Meagan was back at prison, with no gifts or family by her side.

But at least the birth wasn't as traumatic as it could have been. From what he understood, the State of California had banned the use of leg irons, waist chains or handcuffs behind the body on female inmates during labor, delivery or recovery. Still, it broke him to think of Meagan doing this alone. He remembered how she used to trail around the house, carrying her dolls by their hair. Not the best representation of motherhood, by any means. But later, after Ella had been born, Meagan treated her dolls with the sweetest of care.

"May I see your guardianship papers?" Joanne asked, pulling him back to the moment.

"Yes, of course." He gave them to her. He didn't doubt that she'd been through this before. She seemed to know the drill.

She got the clerical procedure under way, and once his identification was verified and forms were signed, he and Candy were asked to wait for the baby to be brought out to them.

The waiting room was a corner setup, with cushioned chairs and a TV on the wall with the sound on mute. No one was there, except for them. Candy sat beside him, with the diaper bag on the other side of her.

From his vantage point, he could see another of those tree murals peeking out from a nearby corner. "I hope they don't make us wait too long."

"They won't," she replied.

She was right. A few minutes later, Joanne came down the hall with a toothy smile. She pushed a bassinet that was fixed atop a stainless-steel cart, its wheels sure and steady.

Simultaneously, Tanner and Candy stood.

"Here she is," the nurse said. "Miss Ivy Ann Quinn."

The baby was nestled into a clear plastic bed, wrapped up like a burrito, with an array of supplies packed in the shelves below her.

Tanner peered down at his niece, preparing to see her for the very first time. She was awake and making kittenish sounds, but she didn't seem like a superhero in the making. She looked more like an extraterrestrial, with her fluffy dark hair and cone-shaped head. He assumed it wasn't anything to worry about; otherwise they wouldn't be releasing her from the hospital. But he couldn't be sure.

"She's beautiful," Candy said, going misty-eyed. "I can't wait to cuddle her."

"Then here you go." Joanne lifted the infant and placed her in Candy's willing arms.

They were a perfect fit, Tanner thought. The nanny and the newborn. He smiled, feeling all warm and weird inside. But insanely nervous, too, just as he'd been all along.

Was the baby looking at Candy? He couldn't tell. His niece seemed a tad cross-eyed. Was that common? Would it go away? Now he wished he had finished those dang books and been more prepared for what to expect. But he wasn't about to point out Ivy's flaws, not when the women were cooing over her perfection. When the nurse put a pink beanie on the baby's coned head, Candy marveled at how cute she looked in it.

He thought it was cute, too. But he kept his opinion to himself. What if she had to wear hats for the rest of her life? That didn't seem fair.

Once it was time to leave, he took charge of the supplies, gathering everything together. He slung the diaper bag over his arm, too. Candy carried Ivy, and they headed home.

With the little alien who'd been entrusted to Tanner.

From the moment Candy held Ivy, she'd fallen instantly in love, and now she was settled into the big padded rocker in the nursery, cradling the baby in her arms.

Meagan's baby, she reminded herself. The newborn swaddled against her belonged to someone else. Yet

Candy had committed the next two years of her life to this precious child.

Tanner sat on the daybed, watching her. The situation seemed surreal. Never had she imagined sharing a child with her first boyfriend. Even if an angel had flown down from heaven and told her this would be happening, she might not have believed it.

And what angel would have done that? Ella? Tanner had told her that Meagan thought of their lost sister as an angel.

Did that make Candy's lost baby an angel, too?

She glanced over at Tanner. He hadn't said much since they'd gotten home. Mostly he just shadowed her and the baby.

"Do you want to hold Ivy?" she asked.

"Not yet."

"She's going to need to be fed again soon." Candy had already given her a bottle earlier. She'd changed diapers, too. He hadn't done anything, except look like a panicked new uncle. "You should feed her this time."

"That's okay. You can do it."

"You're going to have to learn to care for her, Tanner."

"I know, but it's only the first day."

"I have classes two nights a week, and you'll be watching her by yourself while I'm gone. That's going to bite you in the butt if you're not ready for it."

He rose from his spot on the daybed, but he didn't come any closer. "I'll just observe what you're doing for now."

"Come on, give it a try and hold her."

"What if she cries the minute I take her?"

"It'll be fine." Candy got up, offering him the rocker. "Just relax, and I'll put her in your arms."

"I don't want to do anything to upset her."

"You won't." Not with how cautiously he was behaving.

He sat in the rocker, looking apprehensive. But he looked strong and capable, too, surrounded by the magic they'd created in this room. Castles, winged horses and unicorns. And falling stars, she thought, the most important ingredient of all.

She transferred Ivy into his arms, and he reacted automatically, protecting her head and neck.

"See?" Candy said, a lump forming in her throat. "A piece of cake. No tears, no problems. You've got this."

He touched his niece's hand, tracing the tininess of it, and she reacted to the stimuli, wrapping her fingers around one of his.

He flashed a proud smile. "Look at that. She's holding on to me already."

"Yes, she most certainly is." Seeing him with Ivy made her long even more for what she'd lost. But she knew she shouldn't be thinking about that, so she focused on how wonderful he and Ivy were together.

He skimmed the infant's cheek, ever so lightly. Then he glanced up and whispered, "Why is the top of her head shaped like a cone?"

Candy smiled at his question. Had he lowered his voice to keep Ivy from hearing him? Was he concerned that his niece was going to think he was criticizing her, even if she was too young to comprehend his words?

She replied, "That happens to lots of newborns when they pass through the birth canal. Some are just more pronounced than others." And poor little Ivy's was particularly pointy. "It should round in the next day or so."

"I figured it must be okay, but I wasn't sure. Can you imagine how other kids would pick on her if it never went away?" He gazed down at the bundle in his arms. "I don't want anyone to hurt my little girl. Not ever."

His little girl. The reference tugged desperately at her heart. There he was, slipping into the moment, bonding with Ivy. The very thing Candy hoped would happen.

"Will her eyes clear up, too?" he asked, still speaking in a whisper. "I don't know if you noticed, but they're a bit crossed."

Yes, she'd noticed. And his concern was making him seem like the most amazing man in the world. Husband material. Daddy material. Everything he insisted that he wasn't.

Fighting the feeling, she steadied her breath, warning herself not to go wannabe wife on him.

"Will they?" he asked.

She merely stared at him. "I'm sorry. What?"

"Will her eyes clear up?"

She snapped to attention. "Yes, they will. That's typical in newborns."

"What causes it?"

"I think it's just the development of the nerves and muscles. But in some cases, it's also caused by an extra fold of skin in the inner corners of the eyes that creates a cross-eyed look. But those folds disappear as they grow, so that isn't anything to worry about, either."

"I didn't want to say anything at the hospital, but I probably should have spoken up, just to be certain."

"We're supposed to take her to a pediatrician later this week for her first checkup, and you can talk to him about it, if it makes you feel better. We'll take her to the appointment the hospital set up for us, then later we can use Jude's doctor since he's closer."

"How often will we have to go?"

"Every few months, I think. The doctor will tell us—"

"Waaaaa!" Without warning, Ivy let out a wail that was bigger than she was.

"Oh, shoot!" Tanner wrapped her tighter in his arms, rocking her, jiggling her, trying to make her stop. "Is it my fault? Did I do something wrong?"

"No, no. It's nothing you did." Candy forced herself to remain calm, even if it was the first time the baby had cried. "She probably just needs to eat. I told you it would be time to feed her soon."

"Then you should take her."

"I can't fix her bottle and carry her at the same time. Just hang on, and I'll be right back." He needed to keep holding Ivy, even in the middle of a tear storm. It was simply something he would have to get used to.

Still, she rushed off, nearly bumping into Yogi in the hallway. The dog had surfaced to see what was wrong. Before now, the Lab hadn't seemed concerned about having a newborn in the house.

Between Tanner's anxiety and Ivy's angry wails, Candy knew how Yogi felt. It did seem like an emotional emergency.

"Don't worry, girl," she told her dog. "I've got it under control."

Luckily, the formula was already prepared. All she had to do was remove one of the bottles from the fridge and heat it.

The process took less than five minutes, but it seemed like forever with Ivy screaming for her meal.

Candy returned to the nursery and handed the bottle to Tanner. "You might as well do the honors."

He didn't hesitate. He brought the nipple up to Ivy's mouth, and she latched on to it without a hitch.

Silence, Candy thought, except for the sweet sound of suckling. The baby's tantrum was over. Tanner seemed calmer, too, even if he was staring at the little person in his arms as if making one false move might cause her to go ballistic again—which, of course, she very well could.

"Am I doing this right?" he asked.

"Yes. Absolutely." Candy stood back and watched. He was cradling his niece in a semi-upright position and angling the bottle so the milk filled the nipple, keeping Ivy's chances of getting a tummy ache down to a minimum. Regardless of how overwhelmed he was, he had caregiver instincts.

For the duration of the feeding, he didn't take his eyes off of the baby or the bottle.

But once she stopped nursing, he looked up and asked, "What do I do now? I think she's full."

"You need to burp her."

"I have no idea how to do that."

"I can teach you." She draped a small pastel-printed towel over his shoulder. "This is in case she spits up," she told him, much too aware of the striking contrast it made against the rugged fabric of his shirt. Even with a little infant cozy in his arms, he seemed dark and wild, with his piercing gray eyes and masculine vibe.

He shot the towel a suspicious glance. "What if she does more than spits up? What if she full-on pukes?"

Candy bit back a smile. "Then it will be your introduction to baby barf. But let's hope that doesn't happen."

"No kidding."

"You're doing great, Tanner. Truly, you are." So well, she had to keep reminding herself not to get husband designs on him. But before she dwelled too deeply on that, she concentrated on the child in their care. "Lift her up and hold her firmly against your shoulder, then pat her back. But be sure to support her with your other arm."

"I feel like I'm going to hurt her, moving her around like this."

"She's a perfectly healthy baby, and there's no reason for you to worry about something as natural as burping her."

"Okay. Here goes." He followed the directions, going step by step. But nothing happened.

"Try it again," Candy said. "You can use a rubbing motion, too, and see if that works."

Keeping Ivy propped against his shoulder, he did as he was told, but it didn't produce the desired results.

"Is this how you burped her?" he asked, after several more failed attempts. "Did it work for you?"

"Yes. But there are other methods. Sometimes the same one doesn't work the next time around." She suggested that he put the baby facedown on his lap.

He tried that position, and as cute as Ivy looked stretched across him in her drawstring nightgown, with her wispy hair poking straight up, it was to no avail.

He patted. He rubbed. He struck out.

"Maybe she doesn't have any gas," he said.

"Oh, it's in there. Bottle-fed newborns tend to swallow more air than the ones who are breast-fed. Besides, her stomach is only about the size of a golf ball. She can't keep air and food in there at the same time."

"All right, then. What's the next method?" He seemed determined to make it happen.

Candy coached him along. "Sit her up on your lap and lean her forward, but make sure her neck and head are supported, like you've been doing. Then once you have her in place, you can give it another go."

He made the switch, and after applying a few circular pats, he got what he wanted. His niece burped. But it wasn't a delicate little sound of relief. She belched like a truck driver after too many beers.

In the silence that followed, Candy looked at Tanner, and they burst out laughing.

"I guess she told us." He grabbed the towel from his shoulder and wiped a dribble of milky spit from the infant's mouth.

"Do you want me to take her now?" she asked, in case he was ready for a break.

"No. That's okay. I've got her." He lifted Ivy back into his arms and rocked her, content with a job well-done.

Chapter Eleven

Bedtime presented a problem. As the time got closer, Tanner became anxious again. Candy should have expected as much.

Ivy had been taking catnaps since they'd brought her home, dozing in their arms or napping in the cradle that they moved from room to room, where they could watch her. But putting her down for the night was a major ordeal for Tanner.

"I think I should sleep in the nursery," he said.

"Instead of me sleeping in there?"

"No. I think both of us should."

She empathized with how protective he was, but she didn't want him driving himself crazy. Nor did she want to share a room with him, even with a baby between them.

For now, she and Tanner were in the living room

in front of the TV, with his niece just a few feet away, nestled in the cradle.

"Just let me sleep in the nursery by myself," she said. "I'll take excellent care of her. Falling Star will keep her safe, too," she added, hoping to appeal to his Cheyenne side. "He'll catch her before she falls. He'll keep the monsters away."

"That's a lovely sentiment. But you're not going to talk me out of this."

She tried another tactic. "There's not enough room for all of us." The daybed was only big enough for one adult. Not that she would allow Tanner to sleep with her anyway. But it still didn't make sense. "Where are you going to bunk down?"

"I'll crash out on the floor in a sleeping bag."

She made a new argument. "Being in the same room defeats the purpose. We'll both wake up when she cries and neither of us will get any sleep."

"That's what lots of other parents do. You told me that yourself. They keep their newborns in their rooms with them."

"Need I remind you that we're not the parents?"

"Come on, Candy. You know that I wasn't implying that we were. Besides, this isn't going to be anything like that."

"Then what's it going to be like?"

"Just two people looking after a kid. I'll probably be up most of the night anyway. I'm going to read those books so I can get caught on up on this baby stuff."

"It will be too dim in there for that. Ivy's night-light isn't intended for reading. And if you keep the main light on, it will shine in my eyes."

"My e-reader has a light attached to it. It won't bother you."

Apparently he had an answer for everything. "All right. We'll do it your way. But just for tonight."

He made a shooing motion. "Go get dressed for bed. Then I'll get ready when you're done."

Obviously they were taking turns so one of them would be available to keep an eye on Ivy. Of course, at the moment, the baby was wide-awake, sucking on a pacifier and completely unaware that her uncle was being neurotic.

"Go." He shooed her again.

"Okay, okay." She did as he demanded. But she didn't put on her usual pajamas. She went for a modest ensemble of yoga pants and an oversize T-shirt. No way was she going to sleep in the same room with him without being completely covered.

After she brushed her teeth, washed her face and put her hair in a loose ponytail, she returned to him.

He gave her a curious glance. "What's with the baggy top?"

"I'm comfy this way."

He shot her a silly grin. "You're just trying to look less enticing."

"Shut up, Tanner." She didn't need to be called out by him. "At least I have the good sense to be proper."

He shrugged and left to do his thing. While he was gone, she touched Ivy's chubby cheek. Just being near the baby made her heart bubble.

As for the uncle...

He was one gorgeous heap of trouble. He came back looking like an athlete in a magazine ad, wearing a pair of sweat shorts.

Fighting the urge to stare, to admire every ridge and plane, every muscle, every tall, dark part of him, she glanced away. She couldn't reprimand him for wearing shorts, but to her, it didn't seem much different from last night when he'd been in his underwear.

The less fuss she made about his partial state of undress, the less important it would become. She would just have to get used to seeing him half-clothed.

Without commenting on his attire, she removed Ivy from the cradle and carried her into the nursery.

Tanner got his sleeping bag and spread it out on the floor, near the daybed.

She placed Ivy in the crib and both of them gazed lovingly at her. Like new parents. Like everything they weren't supposed to be. Was she going to have to get used to that, too?

He asked, "Did you turn on the monitor?"

"Yes. I made sure the settings were correct, too." Not only did it detect sounds, the sensor pad that went under the mattress was designed to set off an alarm if no movement or no breathing was detected.

He said, "I don't even know if they made that type of monitor when Ella was born. If they did, my family didn't have one." He paused. "I hope it works as well as it's supposed to."

She tried to reassure him. "Dana and Eric never had any trouble with theirs."

"We still have to be careful not to put Ivy on her stomach."

"I know." According to the experts, a primary risk factor in SIDS was babies sleeping on their stomachs. But rather than dwell on that, she said, "She hasn't cried much."

"No, but when she does, boy can she scream." He moved closer to the crib. "She really is beautiful, isn't she?"

"I thought she was perfect from the moment I first saw her."

"I didn't. She looked like she was from outer space to me, instead of the superhero we talked about. But now I'm thinking that she's a princess who hails from a star, like the way some superheroes are from other planets." A smile stole across his face. "She gets her power from her pointy head. Even when it rounds out, she'll still be a superbaby."

"That's sweet, Tanner." A beautiful story for a beautiful child. Going warm and fuzzy, she studied him from beneath her lashes. Who wouldn't be touched by his imagination?

He leaned over the rail and smoothed his niece's flyaway hair. "What a kid, huh? She's already got me wrapped around those tiny fingers."

"Me, too." She wasn't going to downplay her emotions, not when it came to Ivy. "But that's what babies do to people. I adored my little one as soon as it was conceived."

"I wonder if you would've had a boy or a girl."

"I don't know. I think I would have enjoyed having a girl like Ivy. But a boy like Jude would have been amazing, too."

"Maybe Jude and Ivy will grow up and fall head over heels for each other." He withdrew his hand from the crib. "And maybe they won't."

She didn't know what to say about that. Mostly she was hoping that she didn't fall for Tanner. That those wifely feelings wouldn't keep coming back to haunt her.

He switched on the mobile and let "Twinkle Twinkle Little Star" play. Silent, they watched the device go around, the puffy moons and stars connected to it dancing on strings.

"We should get settled in," Candy said while Ivy drifted off to her theme song. "She's almost out."

Tanner turned off the main light switch, leaving the night-light burning. He climbed into his sleeping bag with his e-reader, and she got into the daybed.

"It's pretty in here like this," he said.

"Yes, it is." As magical as a little girl's room should be. The night-light was shaped like a unicorn, its mane embellished with ribbon and its horn gold and glittery.

She pulled up her covers. While he read with his book light, she closed her eyes. But she couldn't sleep. Knowing he was there, so close, made her want to join him on the floor. But she didn't, of course.

Finally, she dozed off, only to be awakened by the distressed call of an infant crying. But Tanner beat her to it. He picked up his niece and held her in his protective arms.

Candy stumbled into the kitchen to fix the bottle. She could have gone back to bed once the formula was ready, but she stayed up while Tanner fed Ivy.

Afterward, he managed to burp her on the first try, using the upright method. He shifted her into a normal position and said, "I think she's wet."

Candy checked Ivy's diaper. He was right. She even had a damp spot on the back of her nightgown.

They placed her on the changing table, and together they tended to the princess who'd appeared in their lives.

But once they returned her to the cushioned comfort

of her crib, they just stood there, caught in a moonlit moment.

In the dimness of the nursery, with the baby making soft sounds, they could've kissed. If they were the actual parents, they might've.

To keep the longing at bay, the feeling of family, Candy moved away from him. But it didn't do any good.

She wanted Ivy's uncle. In the most romantic way possible.

Three weeks had passed since they'd brought Ivy home from the hospital and Candy was still struggling with her feelings for Tanner. And she didn't have a clue what to do about it.

She gazed absently at the ingredients on the kitchen counter. She was preparing dinner for when Tanner got home from work. Ivy was nearby, in the dining room, nestled in her cradle. But the three of them being in the same house together was subject to change. The guesthouse was in the process of being remodeled and as soon as it was complete, Candy would be staying there.

Still, she doubted that moving across the yard was going to help. Her attraction to Tanner wasn't going to magically disappear.

He was all she thought about, not just in wifely ways, but in wild, sexy ways, too. She was even starting to have fantasies about cracking open that bottle of tequila with him.

The innocent girl and the dangerous boy.

If she did something like that, would it cure her of what ailed her? Would she stop imagining him as her husband?

Candy was so confused, she could hardly think straight.

Things were getting complicated all the way around, even with Meagan. They'd been keeping in touch with Tanner's sister over the phone, and she wasn't doing well. In fact, the doctor at the prison had diagnosed her with postpartum depression. They were offering her treatment, but she didn't seem receptive to it. Mostly, she was behaving as if Ivy didn't really belong to her.

That didn't help ease Candy's concerns. She wanted Meagan to embrace her daughter. Tanner, of course, wanted that, too.

They'd been sending all sorts of pictures of Ivy to her. They'd even ordered a baby-safe ink kit so they could make handprints and footprints, tracking Ivy's growth, trying to do whatever they could to keep Meagan in the fold.

Candy returned to the food preparation. She'd found a recipe for a cheese enchilada casserole that sounded good. She'd taken to making vegetarian meals that both she and Tanner could eat, often adding meat for him on the side.

While she spooned the sauce onto the bottom of the pan, her mind wandered back to her dilemma. If she gave in to her fantasies and made wild love with Tanner, she couldn't regret it afterward. Or get emotional. Or pine for more. She couldn't let it backfire.

She needed to be sure that she could handle being his lover. That if they tumbled into bed together, she wouldn't start thinking of it as a marital bed.

So what did that mean? That she actually might do this? At the moment, she didn't know. But now that the seed had been planted, she couldn't deny that it intrigued her.

Feeling fluttery inside, Candy placed the tortillas she'd browned in the pan, added more sauce, spread sour cream over it and layered the cheese. She repeated the process, making the casserole thick and hearty. Lastly, she sprinkled the top with olives and jalapeño peppers, knowing Tanner liked his food with a kick.

The same type of kick he liked his women to have? With that in mind, she added more peppers, just in case she decided to let down her innocent guard in the future.

Making sure everything was plenty hot.

Tanner entered the house through the back door, thinking about how much his life had changed. Not only was he learning to function on less sleep, he was trying to adjust to the arrangement he was in.

He and Candy had been sharing the responsibility of taking care of the baby. Depending on their schedules, they rotated their nights in the nursery. He knew better than to insist on staying in there together again. That was just too dang intimate and something he couldn't handle, not without wanting to turn the nanny into his lover.

They'd agreed that soon it would be time to let Ivy sleep alone in her room, using the monitor to wake them up when she cried. Either way, they would keep their nights separate. It wouldn't matter, though, not if their attraction continued to get in the way.

He walked into the living room, where Candy and Ivy and Yogi were waiting for him.

Well, the woman was, anyway. The baby was in her cradle, sucking on a purple pacifier, and the Lab was protecting the kid, like the watchdog she was fast becoming.

This part was weird for him, almost as if he was coming home to his family. He could smell dinner in the oven, and the aroma was alluringly spicy.

As much as he appreciated Candy's delicious meals, none of this felt quite right. None of it seemed normal. Yet he wasn't looking forward to her moving into the guesthouse, either. Strange as all of this was, he would miss her company.

"Guess what came in the mail?" she asked.

"I have no idea." He pulled off his boots and dropped them where he stood. He wasn't the tidiest guy when he first got home. He had the tendency to leave things where they lay. "So why don't you tell me what came in?"

"The baby-safe ink kit we ordered."

"Really?" he reacted like a new dad and chastised himself for it. They'd bought the kit to make Ivy's handprints and footprints to give to Meagan, not for him to feel fatherly. Still, he was curious to use it. "Did you open it?"

She nodded. "It seems pretty cool."

He dragged a hand through his hair. "I wish Meagan was doing better."

"At least the prison doctor isn't ignoring her symptoms."

"I'm grateful that they're trying to help her." Postpartum depression, he'd learned, was common with women in stressful situations. It only stood to reason that his inmate sister would be subject to it. The "baby blues" consisted of mood swings and crying spells that faded quickly. But the more severe symptoms, like Meagan's, lasted longer and required treatment. "Maybe the ink prints will help cheer her up," he said. "Or maybe it will just be another reminder that she'll be missing out on the first two years of her daughter's life."

"She's going to get better, Tanner. It's just going to take a little time."

"I'll be glad when we take the baby to see her." He walked over to Ivy and glanced down at her. "There's no way she can reject that little face in person." He looked up. "Is there?"

"I don't know how she's going to react. I guess it depends on how effective her treatment is by then. Meagan is struggling to cope with the situation she's in, trying to combat the ache of loving a baby who was taken away from her."

"I knew it was going to be tough, but I hadn't counted on her being so depressed."

"It happens to lots of new mothers. Your sister isn't alone in this." She set his boots off to the side. "I've heard that postpartum can happen to new fathers, too."

Perplexed, he made a face. "How is that even possible?"

"Depression comes in all forms, and having babies can be overwhelming to everyone who's involved."

"I can't argue with that." He scooped Ivy into his arms. "This one has caused me tremendous amounts of anxiety. But she's my sweetheart, too."

"I love seeing how close you are to her."

"That's because she's the best princess ever." He removed Ivy's socks and wiggled her toes. "Look at those pint-size piggies, just itching to get inked."

Wanting to share the baby with Candy, he went over to her. She smiled and joined him in playing with Ivy's feet.

And then he realized his mistake.

He and Candy were only inches apart, with Ivy pressed lovingly between them. He'd just trapped himself in one of those tenderly troubling moments, making him and the nanny seem like the baby's parents.

He stepped back, putting a bit of distance between them. But it didn't help. That cozy feeling was still there, dragging both of them under its uncomfortably romantic spell.

Eager to get away from the house, Candy spent a much-needed afternoon with Dana. They sat in Dana's living room, with the kids napping nearby. Jude had conked out on the floor with his toys, and Ivy was in a portable crib.

Even amid the silence of sleeping children, Candy's thoughts were running a mile a minute. She needed to confide in Dana, to let her emotions out. Because with each day that churned by, her feelings were becoming too much to bear.

"I don't know how much longer I can do this," Candy said.

Dana cocked her head. "Do what?"

"Keep getting tangled up in domestic situations with Tanner. But I've been considering a solution." She took a deep breath, expelling the air in her lungs. "I've been thinking of being with him."

The blonde leaned forward. "You mean sleeping with him?"

Candy nodded. "I was thinking that we could have an affair, of sorts. That if we become lovers, or friends with benefits, as it were, it'll relieve the sexual tension and make our attraction to each other more bearable.

Plus, I'm hoping that once we become lovers, it will make me stop feeling so wifely when I'm around him. That having a wild-and-free affair with him will cancel out the domestic vibe that keeps cropping up."

Dana appeared to be mulling it over. Then she said, "That sounds great, as long as it doesn't have an adverse effect on you."

"I've considered that it could backfire. But to be honest, I'm getting tired of being such a good girl. I want to know what it feels like to be free, to unleash my spirit, to do something I've never done before. I spent all those years being committed to Vince, and where did it get me?"

"Divorced?" Dana asked.

"Exactly. But if I do this with Tanner, there won't be any expectation of us planning a life together. I'll be going into it with my eyes open." Big and wide, she thought. "I can learn to be a new kind of woman. Someone who throws caution to the wind."

"Are you sure about this, Candy? I mean, honestly, what if curling up in bed with him makes you feel more attached? Even more like his wife?"

"I'm well aware that something like that could happen, considering my character and how traditional I've always been. But I'm going to do my best to control those types of feelings. Like I said, I really want to learn to be a new kind of woman and not get so dang attached all the time. I think it would be good for me to have my first affair, and especially with Tanner. He's the perfect guy for it."

"It sounds like you've already made up your mind."

"It does, doesn't it?" She put a hand against her heart, trying to stop it from beating too fast. "But maybe it was inevitable, me making a decision like this. I mean, how long can you want someone without giving in to those types of desires?"

Dana grinned. "Not long, it seems."

Candy continued to rationalize. "At least I'm giving it some thought and running it past you, instead of acting on pure impulse."

"I totally agree. This is your method of making it work. Mine was to climb into bed with Eric the first night. But I've never been cautious about exploring new and adventurous things."

Candy's adventurous side was just starting to unfold. Was she really going to be with Tanner? Was it really going to happen?

"When are you going to seduce him?"

Her pulse leaped. "What?"

"That's your plan, isn't it? To slip into his room one night and seduce him?"

"Actually, I was thinking more along the lines of discussing it with him."

"Really?" Dana just stared at her.

"That will be easier for me. Besides, we're used to talking things out. That's part of what our friendship has been based on."

"Then go for it, sweetie. Sit him down and tell him how you feel."

It did sound a little strange, considering the subject matter. But Candy was only able to take her free spirit so far. She needed to explain to Tanner how this decision came to be.

"He said from the beginning that people were either going to mistake us as Ivy's parents or assume that we were lovers. Of course, we'll still be taking care of Ivy.

But if this works out the way it should, at least those parental-type moments will stop creeping into it."

Dana glanced at the children. "Speaking of Ivy, how is Tanner doing with her? Is he less afraid of the SIDS issue?"

"He's definitely getting there. It helps for him to keep thinking of Ivy as a princess from a star. It makes her seem less breakable to him. The monitor is starting to give him a measure of comfort, too. He likes carrying around the portable receiver and turning up the volume to hear the rhythm of her breathing. He's still over-protective, but, overall, he's made tremendous strides. Neither of us is sleeping in the nursery anymore."

"I'm glad he's less anxious than he was before. It's not healthy to obsess about negative things. And she certainly is an adorable baby. He brags to Eric about her all the time."

Candy smiled. "He's the proudest uncle ever. He's good at everything, even changing dirty diapers. Not that he hasn't gagged a few times." She laughed. "But after he cleans her up, he parades her around like royalty."

"That's nice to hear. And cute, too." Dana laughed a bit, as well. Then she asked, "When do you plan to talk to him about the two of you?"

That was the million-dollar question. "I don't know. There's a lot going on right now, with Meagan's depression and all."

"That poor girl. Is it any wonder she feels the way she does? I would die if I couldn't keep Jude with me. Postpartum or not, that would cause most women to be depressed."

"I know." It made Candy sad, knowing that Meagan was suffering. "We'll be taking the baby to see her next week. But we have no idea how it will affect her."

"I hope the visit goes well, but you should probably wait until it's over before you talk to Tanner. It'll be better to approach that discussion with a clear head."

"I agree. The most important thing right now is Meagan and the baby. But I still need to be prepared to talk to Tanner. I hope I'm not a nervous wreck when the time comes."

Dana sent her a warm smile. "Just say it when it feels right."

"I will. But like you said, for now, I'm going to focus on the visit with Meagan."

And do what she could to make that right.

Chapter Twelve

It was taking Candy forever to get ready for their visit with Meagan. They still had plenty of time, but Tanner just wanted to get this day over with.

Would Meagan be as detached in person as she'd seemed on the phone? He remembered how unresponsive his mom had been after Ella died. Except that Meagan's baby was alive and well, and the comparison made him feel sick. Granted, his sister was in prison, and that sucked. But when it came to Ivy, she should be happy, not sad. She should be working toward her rehabilitation so she could have a future with her child instead of withdrawing from the world. But in spite of what he thought, Meagan's depression was real, and he couldn't fault her for it.

Finally, Candy entered the nursery, where he and the baby were, and he appreciated the sight of her.

"Sorry it took me so long," she said. "I kept going over the list you gave me with the attire restrictions, making sure I didn't violate it. Some of the color schemes that aren't allowed threw me."

He knew what she meant. Not only did you have to be careful not to wear colors that the inmates wore, you couldn't wear clothing that resembled the custodial staff's, either.

"You chose well," he said. She'd donned a modest dress and flat shoes. Her makeup was minimal, and she was devoid of jewelry.

"Thank you." She smiled at Ivy, whom he was holding on his lap. "Did you bathe her?"

"Yep. She's all clean. But we need to put her in something cute." For now all the kid was wearing was a diaper.

She went over to the baby's closet and looked through it. "How about this?" She held up a lace-trimmed romper. "Or this?" A purple dress that looked like a tutu. "Or we can put her in something a bit more casual." She directed his attention to a bodysuit with bumblebees on it.

"I don't know. What do you think?" He wasn't confident in making the decision. Children's fashion wasn't his forte. But he wanted Ivy to look spiffy when she saw her mama. Ivy was his little star, his perfect princess, and he wanted her to shine.

"Let's do the romper," Candy said. "It's sweet and girlie, but not too fussy. We're only allowed to pack one extra change of clothes for her. So I think we should go for the jumpsuit as our backup, just to keep it simple."

While she gathered the outfits, he rocked Ivy on his lap. He was getting so used to rocking the baby, sometimes he swayed back and forth, even when he didn't have her in his arms. He'd seen Candy do that sometimes, too. He figured it was a parental reflex, which was troubling in and of itself. Things like that made him feel like Ivy's daddy instead of her guardian, which put Candy in the mommy role, too.

"Did I tell you that Meagan tried to postpone this visit?" he asked.

She turned to face him, a frown marring her pretty features. "No, you didn't mention that. What made her change her mind?"

"I insisted that we were coming, and she caved in and accepted it."

"Maybe that's a good sign, rather than her fighting you on it."

He hoped so, but there were no guarantees. He didn't know what to expect when it came to his sister.

While he fell silent, Candy began packing the diaper bag for their trip, making sure she followed the guidelines of what they were permitted to carry with them.

Even the rules about the bag itself were specific. This one was clear plastic, like the purse Candy had to use.

Tanner watched as she selected the permissible items: one transparent pacifier, one burp cloth, six disposable diapers, one small blanket and a sealed package of wipes.

As for the baby's food, they would be bringing two clear bottles filled with premade formula.

She looked up and said, "I'm going to grab some extra diapers and leave them in the truck. It's too long a trip to be caught with such minimal supplies." She then asked, "So what's it going to be like when we first get there?"

"You mean the security stuff?"

She nodded.

He replied, "Sometimes the initial processing takes a while, depending on how many visitors are there. Once we get into the building, we'll have to fill out our passes, with Meagan's name and CDCR number, along with our names, addresses, signatures and relationship to her. I'm her brother, of course, and you'd be considered a friend."

"Will Ivy need a pass?"

"Yes. I'll be filling hers out. I have to bring her birth certificate and my guardianship papers, too." He added, "Once our passes are approved, we'll be searched in a method that's similar to airport security, with a conveyor belt and metal detectors."

"Will Ivy be exposed to the detector?"

"Yes, but since she's too young to walk through it, I'll be instructed to carry her." On previous visits, he'd seen other guardians and parents taking their babies and toddlers through. "After that, we'll go to the visiting room or area that's been assigned to us, show the staff on duty our passes and wait for Meagan to arrive. Sometimes Meagan and I sit outside on the patio, when it's available, but I think we should stay indoors with Ivy. Either way, everything will be under surveillance, manned by correctional officers and camera equipment."

Candy sighed. "No wonder your sister is so reluctant to have us bring Ivy there."

"It's not going to be easy. But it's important for Meagan to see Ivy." He shifted his niece on his lap. She was kicking her feet in that infant way of hers. She was flapping her arms, too, like a fledging struggling to take flight. "I can't wait for her to smile."

"Meagan?"

"Actually, I was talking about Ivy. I know what Meagan looks like when she smiles. But not this little one." He poked her rounded belly. "I'm anxious to see how it transforms her."

"Most babies smile between six and eight weeks old, but sometimes it can happen sooner."

"When did Jude first smile?"

"At about six weeks. It was a thrill every time it happened. And now he smiles and laughs all the time."

He didn't recall Ella's first smile, but he did remember how cute she looked when she grinned, reacting to the funny faces he used to make at her. "When Ivy first does it, it's probably going to melt the hell out of my heart."

"Mine, too." She already seemed a little dreamy. "Plus all of the other milestones like sitting up by herself, crawling, waving bye-bye, eating finger foods, standing, walking and saying her first word."

"What do you think her first word will be?"

"Usually it's *mama* or *dada.*"

He frowned, concerned about where those words might lead. "We can't let her call us by those names. That wouldn't be right."

"We won't." She blew out a choppy breath, recovering from her dreaminess, from the maternal aura that had been surrounding her. "We'll help her come up with something else for us. Maybe Canny and Tanny, like Jude does."

"That will work." He could still feel himself frowning. "We can't steal Meagan's child from her. Even with how messed up my sister is right now, it doesn't change the fact that Ivy belongs to her."

"I know." She reached for the baby, preparing to dress her for the prison. "Believe me, I know."

Candy noticed how distant Meagan was, barely interacting with the baby. Even though Meagan was permitted a contact visit, giving her the right to hold her child, the most she'd done was touch Ivy's hand.

"She hardly ever cries," Tanner said.

"That's good," Meagan replied in a sad voice.

"I tell her every day that you love her," Candy put in.

Meagan glanced up, her eyes dark with pain. "I do love her. But she's not going to know me as her mother." She studied Candy. "You're going to be more like her mom. You're the one who will be there every day."

"I'm the nanny," Candy quickly responded. "And you're her mom. You being in here doesn't change that."

"Yes, it does. I don't want my daughter to keep coming here, seeing me like this. It'll be better for her to have a normal life with you and Tanner and just leave me out of it."

Her brother spoke up. "There's no way we're doing that. Candy and I aren't a couple, and we're not becoming Ivy's parents. We were just saying that right before we came here. We're not stealing your child from you."

"You wouldn't be stealing her. I'd be letting you have her." She divided her gaze between them. "And you seem like a couple to me."

He shook his head. "Well, we aren't."

"Maybe you should be." She gave her brother a pointed look. "I can tell you're into each other."

"Don't you dare try to play matchmaker. You know darned well I'm not the commitment type." He fidgeted in his seat. "Candy wants to settle down at some point, and someday she will. She'll find another guy and marry him and have kids of her own. But Ivy is your baby, Meagan. *Yours.*"

Candy interjected. How could she not, with everything Tanner had just said? "He's right, honey. She's your daughter."

Meagan didn't reply. She just sat there, looking despondent in her stiff uniform and barely combed hair. Such a far cry from the bouncy eight-year-old Candy remembered.

The discomfort was thick enough to cut with a machete. Between the three of them, no one seemed to know what to do or what to say.

Then Tanner asked his sister, "How is your treatment going?"

She shrugged. "It's not going to change me being in here and Ivy being out there."

Candy said, "No, it won't. But once you start feeling better, it will change how you react to your situation."

"I'd feel better if you guys became a couple and agreed to keep Ivy." She gazed at her daughter. "I can tell how attached she is to both of you already. And you even look like you could be her parents."

"Stop saying that kind of stuff." Tanner's frustration mounted. "We're not claiming Ivy as our own. Our focus is for you to get well." He softened his voice. "Your baby girl needs you, sis."

"But I'm such a screwup."

"Lots of people make mistakes." He took her hand. "I want for you to prove to me that you can be strong and get well for your daughter. Please, Meagan. Don't cop out. At least accept the help they're giving you."

Her voice hitched. "I'll try to feel better. But it's just so hard, being an absentee parent."

"Lots of other moms are in here, too." Tanner gestured to the families who surrounded them. "And in two years, you'll be home with your daughter. This isn't going to be forever."

Ivy started to fuss and Candy reached into the diaper bag for the pacifier and popped it into her mouth, calming her right down. "Do you want to hold her?" she asked Meagan. "Just for a minute?"

The reluctant mother shook her head. "Maybe next time."

"We can bring her back next week," Tanner said.

"That's too soon. I need more time." She looked at Candy. "Just be her mom for now, okay?"

Candy's heart clenched. "How about if I just be her really good, really loving nanny?"

"I'm still going to think of you as her mom." She turned to Tanner. "And you as her dad. *Tshe-hestovestse.*"

She repeated the Cheyenne word that meant both father and uncle.

And that was where the visit came to an end. Their time had run out, with Meagan foisting parenthood on them. Then, just as quickly, she was escorted away with the rest of the lost and lonely inmates.

In the evening, Tanner did his damnedest to decompress. He and Candy had gotten Chinese takeout for dinner, and he'd already set the food up on the coffee table in front of the TV. But for now, they were putting the baby down for the night. They took turns kissing her forehead, and then he placed her in the crib.

Candy turned on the mobile, which began playing the lullaby. "She's wiped out."

"It's been an exhausting day. Truthfully, I don't think I could handle taking her to the prison every week. What an ordeal that was. Can you believe that stuff Meagan said?"

"She's just having a tough time."

"I understand how mixed-up she is. But we don't need her trying to push us into becoming parents." It was bad enough that he'd been stressing about him and Candy seeming like a couple without his sister making a big issue out of it.

"That was uncomfortable for me, too."

"I know. I could tell." He moved away from the crib and glanced back at Ivy. "At least the baby is too young to understand. I'd hate for her to be knowingly caught up in all of this."

Candy turned down the light, and they left the room, taking a portable receiver with them so the activity from the nursery would be within earshot.

He sat on sofa, and she joined him, with the food in front of them. Lobster lo mein for him and steamed vegetables for her.

He tore open the wrapper the disposable chopsticks came in, then broke the wooden utensils apart, preparing to eat his lo mein. "I wonder what our fortune cookies are going to say. Something good, I hope. I really need some positive news."

"We can read them after we finish our meals. It would be cheating to look at them ahead of time."

"I wasn't suggesting that we sneak a peek." Not that it mattered anyway. He didn't believe that a little slip of paper, with a factory-printed fortune, was going to change his life.

She turned on the TV. "What do you want to watch?"

"You can choose something." He was already busy chopsticking his meal. He'd always thought that part of the fun of Asian cuisine was the clumsiness that went with not using a fork. Or the finesse, if you were good at it.

"Why don't we stream a movie?"

"That's fine. I don't care what it is, as long as it doesn't involve any prison scenes."

She shot him a goofy smile. "So that leaves out *The Shawshank Redemption* or *The Green Mile* or *Escape from Alcatraz*?"

He laughed. He appreciated that she was making a joke. Humor always made things easier for him. "Don't forget about *The Rock*."

She lifted the lid on her food container. "Or *Jailhouse Rock.*"

Impressed with her clever segue, he leaned over and bumped her shoulder. "Good call. Elvis was the man." He paused, taking his turn. "How about *The Longest Yard*? The original and the remake?"

"Oh, I like those movies." She reached for the plastic fork he'd rejected. "What about *Dead Man Walking*?"

"I'd rather forget that one." As good as it was, the subject matter was too serious for him. He fell silent for a few seconds, his mind going blank. "I can't think of any more offhand, can you?"

"No, I'm sure there are tons of them that we missed."

"Not to mention TV shows."

"Like *Prison Break*?" she asked. "Or *Orange Is the New Black*?"

"Yeah, smarty. Like those." Orange was one of the colors they weren't allowed to wear when they visited the prison. "You still need to pick something that we're actually going to watch."

"How about a classic?" She bumped his arm, the way he'd done to her. "Something from before our time."

"A sappy old movie? What did I get myself into?"

"They weren't all sappy. And I love old movies. They're so big and sweeping and larger-than-life."

"So unrealistic, you mean?"

She rolled her eyes. "Don't be a spoilsport. You told me I could choose, and after the day we had, I'm in the mood for something old-fashioned."

"Okay. Then go for it." He would be all right with a war picture or a maybe a Western, if it didn't have singing cowboys or fake Indians in bad wigs and Hollywood war paint.

While she scanned the classics list, he focused on his chopstick skills.

"Here's one with Cary Grant and Deborah Kerr," she said. "It says it's supposed to be one of the most romantic films of all time."

He stalled in midbite. "A chick flick?" That didn't sound the least bit appealing to him.

"They weren't called chick flicks in those days, and it has a five-star rating."

"What's it about, exactly?" He was only vaguely familiar with Cary Grant, let alone Deborah What's-Her-Name.

She checked the synopsis. "The hero and heroine meet on an ocean liner and fall deeply in love. But they're tempting fate because they're both engaged to other people. They agree to meet at the Empire State

Building six months later to see if they still feel the same way, but a tragic accident prevents their rendezvous, and their lives take an uncertain turn."

"That sounds kind of heavy."

"It does, doesn't it?" She put down the remote. "It's okay if we don't watch it. It was just the title that caught my eye."

He hadn't paid attention to the title. He hadn't looked at the screen. So he glanced up and saw that it was called *An Affair to Remember*. "Now you're just plain confusing me. Why would a title like that interest you?"

"Because I've been thinking about something."

"Something?"

"About us changing the dynamics of our friendship and having an affair." She sucked in her breath. "I want to explore a new side of myself, and I want you to be part of the new me. I already talked to Dana about it because I needed to get it off my chest before I discussed it with you. Dana agreed that I should wait to tell you until after you and I saw Meagan, and—"

"Hold on." He didn't want to hear the anxious details, not until he understood precisely what she meant. "What do you mean you want to explore a new side of yourself?"

"I want to know what it's like to stop being so traditional. So marriage-minded. So innocent."

"But that's who you are, Candy."

"But I don't want to be that girl when I'm with you."

He searched her gaze, scanning the depths of her eyes and the naturally spiky lashes that framed them. "You don't have to change who you are because of me." He wasn't even sure if she could. "Maybe you better rethink this a bit."

"I don't want to rethink it. I want to act on my attraction to you without feeling like your wife."

So she could go off and marry someone else later? "I'm not trying to talk you out of it." Not when she was offering herself to him in such an open and honest way. "But you need to be sure that you're making the right decision."

"I am sure." She kept her gaze riveted to his. "Honestly, I think that this will help me to *not* fall for you. Besides, we need to try to tackle the heat, the palpable tension of wanting each other. Even your sister noticed it."

"Yeah, and with her trying to turn us into a couple. Are you sure that's not what you're trying to do, not even subconsciously?" He had to be absolutely certain of her motives. "Because you know that I wouldn't be able to handle it. That it would freak me out."

"That's not what I'm after. Not even in the back of my mind. I just want to feel hot and sexy. I want to make wild love with you. The kind of lovemaking that will free my soul."

His body went warm. All over. He imagined carrying her straight to his bed and stripping her bare. Naked all the way. But he wasn't going to act impulsively.

"I have an idea," he said. "Why don't we plan a date night? We can ask Eric and Dana to babysit, and I can take you out to dinner, maybe a little dancing—"

"I don't want to go on a date."

He blinked at her. "Why not?"

"Because that seems too traditional. I want to do something crazy. Like go to your apartment at the stables and crack open that bottle of tequila."

"Really?"

"Yes, really," she assured him.

Then he wasn't about to refuse. He would gladly give Candy her independence, right along with the wildness she craved. "If that's what you want, then that's what we'll do."

"Do you think we could do a few body shots? I've never done those before."

"Damned straight we can." He longed to get crazy with her, to teach her how to be wild and dangerously wicked. "But let's not get too drunk that we don't remember what we did." He wanted to remember every kiss, every caress.

"When is this going to happen?" she asked.

"As soon as we can arrange for Dana and Eric to watch Ivy. They can stay here with Jude, if they're okay with that. I'd prefer that Ivy sleep at home, rather than take her over there for an entire night."

"That's going to be a big step for you, Tanner. Letting someone else take care of Ivy, especially all night."

"I know. But I trust Dana and Eric. And I'm trying to learn to stop worrying every time she falls asleep."

She smiled at him. "I'm proud of you for the progress you made. I even told Dana how well you're doing."

"Apparently you tell her everything."

"Sometimes I do. Not always."

"This time you did."

"And now everything is settled." She went back to the TV, searching for something besides the romantic movie to watch. "I'm so glad we got it figured out."

"Me, too." He studied her, thinking how lucky he was to have her as his friend and soon-to-be lover.

After they finished their meals, they broke open their cookies. His fortune read "Accept the next proposition you hear," and hers was "You will take a chance at something in the near future."

They could do little more than laugh at the perfection of the words that had been presented to them.

Intrigued by her, Tanner moved closer, inhaling the sweetness of her skin. The perfume that lingered. The scent of flowers in a sensual mist. "Should I kiss you now for a taste of things to come? Or wait until our first night together?"

She sucked her bottom lip between her teeth. Nibbling. Biting. Which made his zipper go painfully tight.

"Let's wait," she said. "Let's torture ourselves for the heck of it."

Oh, he was being tortured all right. But he loved how the temptation made him feel.

Every hot, thrilling, anticipatory second of it.

Chapter Thirteen

On the day Dana and Eric were available to baby-sit, Tanner was working. Since he was already at the stables, he wouldn't be coming home. Candy was in charge of getting the babysitters settled, and after that she would be meeting Tanner at his apartment.

Nervous excitement filled her with sexy butterflies. She couldn't wait to see him, to let down her hair, to get hot and tipsy.

For her wardrobe, she'd donned a low-cut halter dress with a short hemline, resulting in no bra and lots of leg. Underneath, she wore a pair of lace panties. She'd moisturized her skin with a silky lotion and packed an overnight bag with a change of clothes for the morning. She didn't bring any pajamas. She intended to sleep with Tanner in the buff.

"You look amazing," Dana told her as they stood in the kitchen, filling bottles of Ivy's formula.

"It's going to be the night of my life."

"It absolutely will. And don't worry about anything on the home front. My man and I have got that covered."

"I know Ivy will be safe with you guys." For now, Eric was in the living room with both children. "I can't tell you how much Tanner and I appreciate this."

"I love that you're having your first rendezvous at his apartment."

Her heart bumped in her chest. "Me, too."

Dana put the bottles in the fridge. "Now, say goodbye to the kids and get going."

Candy did just that. She went into the living room and gave Ivy a big loving cuddle. She offered Jude the same affectionate treatment and swept him into her arms.

"Canny," he said, giving her a toddler's noisy kiss.

They separated, and she waved to him on the way out the door. She shot Eric and Dana a quick finger waggle, too.

A short time later, she arrived at the stables and headed for Tanner's place. She entered the office building and took the stairs to his apartment. Already her pulse was fluttering, her body all too aware of itself.

She tried the door, but it was locked. Eager for their night to begin, she knocked.

Tanner appeared, looking fresh from the shower. His thick black hair was damp and falling in short choppy clumps against his forehead. His clothes consisted of a pair of jeans.

Low-slung denims and tousled hair. Damn if he didn't make her mouth water.

"Wow," he said as he checked her out. "You look

beautiful." He paused. "I can't believe you're actually here. You and me. Together like this."

She smiled and nudged him backward, toward the interior of the apartment. "Let me in before I melt all over myself out here."

"Yes, ma'am." He grabbed hold of her, and they stumbled inside, where she dropped her overnight bag.

He didn't waste a second of their precious time. He kissed her hard and fast, the frenzy between them packed with lust. She moaned and met his fervor, tongues tangling and teeth clashing. He'd never kissed her like this when they were younger. Not this desperately.

After he pulled back, he said, "I bought you some roses."

"You did?" Still reeling from the kiss, she asked, "What color?"

"Orange. They mean passion and desire. I wanted to do something special for you, but I didn't want to get too traditional, so I figured that wild-themed flowers would work."

Pleased with his bohemian romanticism, she leaned into him. "Where are they?"

"In the bedroom. But they're rose petals, not the full flowers, so I sprinkled them on the bed." He trailed a finger down her collarbone, toying with the cleavage her dress revealed. "The tequila is in the bedroom, too. On the nightstand, with the salt and lime."

She bumped his fly. He was already hard beneath his zipper. "Can I see the bed?"

His lips quirked into a half smile. "Don't be surprised if I went overboard." He took her hand and led her to his room.

Sweet mercy. *Overboard* was an understatement. The quilt was drawn, revealing a white sheet covered in orange petals.

"I ordered them from a florist," he said. "They sell them by the hundreds."

Unable to resist, she removed her shoes and flung herself on the mattress, scattering the bright foliage. "This is heavenly, Tanner."

"I'm glad you think so. I discovered that orange roses are a cross between yellow and red roses, and the meaning comes from both. Yellow is associated with friendship and red represents love. When you put them together, you get desire that stems from friendship."

She was impressed with his research. "You really thought this through."

"I tried to come up with something that was significant between us, something that mattered."

"It does matter. Thank you." It was wonderfully romantic, but sweetly sensual, too. It almost made his room seem like a honeymoon suite.

A honeymoon suite?

Candy quickly curbed the image. Marriage was supposed to be the last subject on her mind.

Tanner leaned against the cherrywood armoire, his gaze trained on her. "Take off your dress. I want to look at you."

Her heart jumped to her throat. "You are looking at me."

"Don't be coy. You know what I mean."

Yes, she knew. She was stalling to catch her breath. "I need a second."

"No extra seconds allowed. Do it now."

She liked that he'd given her a sexy order. She liked

everything about him. He was her friend, and now he was about to become her lover, just like the orange rose indicated. No husband imaginings, she reminded herself. No dreamy musings.

"Candy," he said. "Your dress."

"I'm doing it now." She reached behind her neck and worked free the tie that held it in place. Once that was undone, the garment slid to her waist. She peeled it off, leaving her topless, her bottom half barely covered by the lace panties.

He stared at her, and she imagined how she looked, 90 percent naked and surrounded by flower petals.

"Damn," he said. "You know how to drive a guy crazy."

He went over to the nightstand, picked up the tequila and broke the seal, opening the bottle.

Candy watched him, waiting to see what came next. Her heart hadn't quit pounding. Her pulse was even thudding between her legs. He knew how to drive a girl crazy, too.

"It's time for a shot," he said. "And I get to go first."

He poured a glass and set it off to the side. Next he lifted a lime wedge and brought it up to her mouth, explaining that she should keep it there, until he was ready for it.

She gripped it between her teeth, and he leaned forward and glided his tongue over one of her breasts, dangerously close to the nipple.

Sweet, sweet sin. She shivered from the want of him.

He sprinkled salt on the damp spot, and when he licked it off, her nipple got in the way, and he tongued that, too.

Every muscle in Candy's body tensed. He added more salt, just for the hell of it, just to tease her.

More licks, more tastes.

Finally, he grabbed the shot glass and drank the tequila. As soon as he swallowed the liquid, he covered her mouth with his and removed the lime.

Roughly. Erotically.

She clawed the rose petals, clutching them in her hands. She'd been celibate for years and now she was playing drinking games with Tanner Quinn.

He ditched the lime and kissed her, the taste of citrus sizzling between them. Candy released the foliage and pulled him down on top of her. They rolled over the bed, body to body, pulse to pulse, still kissing like fiends.

"I'm doing one more shot," he told her. "Then you can take your turn."

She wasn't about to refuse. He could have whatever he wanted, in any order he wanted it.

Once again a lime wedge went in her mouth, but this time he poured a dollop of tequila in her belly button, making her breath catch.

He licked her stomach and sprinkled the salt. After another sexy slash of tongue, he sucked the tequila from her navel.

Keening out a soft moan, Candy thrust her hips. He was toying with the waistband of her panties. But he didn't remove them. He cruised his way up her body and took the lime from her mouth with his.

She wrapped her arms around him and held tight. He discarded the lime, and they kissed, hot and deliciously wet. Nothing had felt so right, so wrong, so wild, so decadent.

So out of character for Candy. But this was the new woman she was becoming. The long-ago girl, leaving her innocence behind. She was making up for lost time, getting free and wild with Tanner. This was exactly what she wanted, what she needed.

"You're so sweet," he said. "And salty."

She smiled, thinking about how generous he'd been with the shaker. "Gee, I wonder why."

"Yeah, I wonder." He looked into her eyes and dusted rose petals out of her hair. "We've got these dang things all over us. Maybe I shouldn't have gone so overboard with them."

"I don't mind. I think it's beautiful." Some of them were stuck to his skin, dotting his big broad chest. "But you're still wearing your pants. That's not fair. If I'm in my underwear, then you should be, too."

He undid the top snap of his jeans. "If you say so." He took her hand and placed it against his fly. "But if you want them off, you should at least open the zipper."

Heavens, yes. She went after the metal teeth with a vengeance. She helped drag the denim down his hips, too. He was wearing the same type of boxers she'd seen him in before.

She admired the darkly dangerous sight of him. His underwear was black and hers was white. Somehow that seemed to make perfect sense.

She sat up. "It's time for me to do my shots."

"You only get two, so make them count."

"I will."

"Then go for it." He kicked back and grinned like the bad boy he was. "I'm all yours."

All hers. She liked the sound of that. Candy slipped a lime wedge into his grinning mouth, and it made him look even more devilish.

She couldn't decide what part of him to salt and lick.

So she hesitated, contemplating her options. He raised his eyebrows, reminding her he was waiting with the lime.

She smiled. "Sorry. My inexperience is showing."

He gestured to the tequila, silently telling her that she'd forgotten to pour herself a shot.

Oops. She got it ready and set it off to the side. Then she went back to her decision. Should she salt his neck, his chest, his stomach...?

She gave his belly button a gander. He had a nice inny. She would definitely save that for the second drink, like he'd done with her.

For her first encounter, she chose his neck. There was something incredibly sexy about doing it so close to his face.

She rolled her tongue along the cords in his throat, giving them both a sensual jolt. She added the salt and licked the passionate hell out of him, filling her senses with his skin.

Completing the process, she drank the tequila, shuddering from the slow burn as it went down, her eyes watering. It was even stronger than she'd assumed it would be.

She took the lime from his mouth, plowing into the kiss that came after it. The long, lingering flavor. The heat. The excitement of being wild with Tanner. They kissed and kissed, wicked pleasure bursting from their pores.

During the belly-button shot, she scraped a nail along his thigh, giving him an extra thrill. He was as aroused as a man could get.

As the last bit of alcohol fired through her blood, she delved into his boxers and felt him up. Closing her fingers around him, she moved up and down, relishing his masculine heat.

He didn't let her play for long. He nudged her hand away and started pushing the rose petals onto the floor.

"What are you doing?" she asked.

"What does it look like I'm doing?" Pieces of orange flew off the bed and floated to the ground. "I'm getting rid of them."

Mesmerized by the falling flowers, she watched him clear the bed. He'd created the romantic ambience, but now he seemed determined to consummate their affair, without anything getting in his way.

Tanner peeled off Candy's panties, anxious to do away with the only scrap of clothing she had left on. Such a pretty wisp of fabric, he thought. He tossed it onto the floor, where it settled into the flower heap.

She smiled at him, looking soft and sweet and glassy-eyed.

"Are you tipsy?" he asked.

"A little."

"Technically, we only had one shot." What she'd taken from his navel wasn't more than a thimble, about the same small amount he'd taken from hers.

"I hardly ever drink. But I think maybe I'm also tipsy from touching you and kissing you and licking your skin." She made a sexy, dreamy sound. "And letting you take my underwear off."

He nuzzled her ear. She still had a few petals in her hair. "I like corrupting you."

"You're good at it."

"I'm glad you think so." Her lipstick was gone. Her

mascara was smeared, too, making catlike rims around her eyes. Even with flawed makeup, she was ravishing.

She tugged at his boxers. "You need to get naked, too."

"I intend to." He removed his underwear, freeing himself. He wanted nothing more than to be inside her. But he held out for more foreplay, putting his mouth between her legs.

He tasted her in the most intimate way, drinking her in, getting intoxicated on the feeling. She was deeper and richer and warmer than the tequila.

She rocked against him, her moans light and breathy and barely audible. He'd never touched a more sensitive woman. She was worth the wait. Seventeen long years of it.

Already he could feel her coming unglued, slowly, like an envelope reacting to steam, its edges unfurling.

She arched and sighed, her eyelashes fluttering.

As her legs tensed, as her stomach muscles quivered, Tanner absorbed her release.

Sweet, silky madness.

He rose up to kiss her, to breathe in the warmth of her orgasm. More than ready, he removed a condom from the nightstand.

He tore into the packet and took out the protection. She watched him put it on. Neither of them could seem to keep their eyes to themselves.

Tanner slid between her legs and buried himself to the hilt. She dragged his face down to hers, and they kissed, the sensation of being together rising like a phoenix from the ashes.

He moved inside her, and they tumbled over the bed

in mutual greed, their mouths desperately fused. She clawed his back and wrapped her legs tighter around him.

Being with her was everything he'd imagined it would be.

They hadn't even turned down the lights. The room was bright, making their union highly visible.

The only darkness was the night outside his windows. The stables with their fences and horses and breezeway barn. The trails in the distance, with the tall timber of trees.

Together, they moved in synchronicity, like dancers on their own private stage. They kept turning, tumbling, until she landed on top.

She sat forward on his lap, riding him with freedom and grace. He watched the way her body arched, the way she tossed her head back.

Lost in the passion, he reared up to claim her mouth, to tug on her hair. He didn't know if she was on the verge of climax. He thought she was, but he couldn't be sure. He was too far gone to know anything except how good she was making him feel.

With his vision blurring, with his heart pumping blood through his veins, he came, hard and fast, his lover's sweet, sugary name spilling roughly from his lips.

Candy slept soundly, warm and snug in Tanner's bed. And in the morning when she awakened, with daylight streaming across her naked skin, she sat up and glanced around.

She was alone in the room. She didn't know where Tanner was, but everything looked the same as they'd left it. The tequila and shot glasses remained on the nightstand and the rose petals were still strewn all over the floor.

She smiled at the memory. What a night. What a glorious, sexy, beautiful night. She could do this for the rest of her life.

No, she told herself. She couldn't. Because it wasn't meant to last. If anything, it would be two years at best. Friends turned lovers, with no strings to trip over.

She glanced up, and suddenly there he was, standing in the doorway like a mirage.

"Hey, sleepyhead," he said. "I got coffee, tea and muffins." He held up a cardboard container with the cups, along with a white paper bag that contained the food.

"That sounds great." She sat a little more forward, pulling the sheet up. It was strange being bare while he was clothed.

He was dressed in jeans, a black T-shirt and Western boots, which she'd come to learn was his most common casual attire.

As he approached her, he tromped right over the flower petals. He might've even walked on her underwear since they were in the pile somewhere.

He said, "Obviously the cup with your name on it is for you. It's chai tea."

"Thank you." She drank coffee on occasion, but mostly she preferred tea.

She kept the lid on her cup, opening the plastic tab and sipping from it. He did the same thing with his coffee.

He opened the bag. "The muffins are blueberry bran. It's the healthiest thing they had. But I doubt it's going to be anything like the ones you make."

"I'm down with blueberry bran." She accepted one of the muffins, along with a napkin. "I need to call Dana and Eric to see how Ivy is."

"I already did that, and she's fine." He sat on the edge of the bed. "She woke up twice during the night, screamed her little head off until they fed her, drank her formula, burped way too loud and went back to sleep."

She laughed. "Sounds like our kid." She quickly corrected herself. "I mean Meagan's kid."

"I know what you meant." He was quick to move past it, too. "This morning, they're taking Ivy outside to carry her around the yard. Jude wants to run around out there, so they figured it would do both kids good to get a little fresh air."

"That's a nice idea."

"I thought so, too. I think Ivy is going to love the lemon tree when she gets older. Your garden is part of the reason I bought the house."

"It's your garden now." His house. His property.

"The flowers and trees will always belong to you, even when you're not living there anymore."

Candy took a shaky breath, the thought of being without him constricting her throat. Yet she was supposed to know better, especially with this free-spirited relationship being her brilliant idea.

Was it a mistake? Was it truly possible for her not to get attached? Had she fooled herself into thinking that she was capable of trying to change her ways, without suffering the consequences?

Heaven help her. It was only the first morning after, and already she was worried that she shouldn't have crawled into bed with him. She needed to get a grip, especially after the way she'd insisted that she could handle it.

He leaned forward, and her pulse jumped. "What are you doing, Tanner?"

"Kissing you." He put his mouth against hers.

She ditched her muffin and pulled him into her arms. She couldn't stop wanting him if she tried. Somehow, someway, she would stick to her original plan and make this work, even if it meant hiding her fretful emotions.

He started battling with his clothes, pulling and yanking at them. Off went his boots, his socks, his shirt. When he got to his jeans, he gave up the fight and left them on, just shoving them down far enough to free himself and use protection.

With another mind-blowing kiss, he was deep inside her, thrusting with beautiful force. She pushed back, meeting his frenzied rhythm, until her mind went blank, right along with her pulsing, pounding, fear-induced heart.

Chapter Fourteen

Over the next few weeks, Candy and Tanner spent countless days and nights together. Her fear of getting attached to him hadn't subsided. It had actually been getting worse. But she kept those feelings to herself, doing her damnedest not to fall in love with him.

She'd graduated to using the *L*-word, desperately hoping that it wouldn't happen.

By now the guesthouse was complete, but she wouldn't be moving in. He'd asked her to stay in the main house with him, making it easier for them to be together, and she'd gone ahead and agreed.

But in light of her struggle, she wondered if that was wise. Why? Because sleeping in his room with him made her feel like his wife? She wasn't supposed to be allowing herself that kind of twisted luxury.

She entered the nursery, where Tanner was sitting

in the rocking chair, reading a nursery rhyme to Ivy. It wasn't important if she didn't understand the story. Talking to babies helped stimulate their minds.

He glanced up. "Hey," he said to Candy, quickly meeting her gaze. Then he paused and asked, "Are you okay?"

Shoot. She smoothed her clothes as if that was the problem. "Don't I look okay?"

"You seem preoccupied. You've seemed that way a lot lately."

Yes, well, if he only knew. "I'm fine."

"I think there's something going on. Come on, what is it?"

She grappled for an excuse. "It's my mom. She's been calling and leaving messages, trying to get me to invite her to come over." At least that was true, even if it wasn't the main thing on Candy's mind. "She says she wants to see the baby and bring her a gift."

"So your mom is softening up a bit, huh?"

"I don't know. Maybe. It's hard to tell with her."

"You should return her calls and arrange a time for her to visit."

"Yes, I suppose I should. But I hope she isn't using the baby gift as an excuse to pry. If she hangs around long enough, she's certainly astute enough to figure out that we're lovers."

"So what's the point of hiding it from her? We're both consenting adults. She's just going to have to accept our relationship for what it is."

He obviously didn't care if her mom uncovered the truth. But no doubt he would care if he discovered how emotional Candy was getting over him.

"Are you working tonight?" he asked, moving on to another subject.

She nodded. "I have a doga class at six." But her thoughts were elsewhere, of course. Trying to shut out her worries, she gazed at the child in his lap. "Is Ivy enjoying her story?"

He glanced down. "She sure is. Aren't you, little star?"

Candy came closer and stood beside the rocker. The baby kicked her feet and reacted to Tanner, shooting him a smile.

Her first smile!

"Oh, wow!" He whipped his head around. "Did you see that? Did you see what she did?"

"Yes." She was as excited as he was. Her pulse was jumping all over the place. "I'm going to go grab my camera. When I get back, say something to her to try to get her to do it again so I can take a picture."

"Okay. This is so cool." He was grinning from ear to ear.

Candy rushed off and returned with her camera. Tanner coaxed the baby into another smile, and they both went batty, with her snapping as many pictures as she could get.

"Let's try it again," he said. "With a video this time, so we can put it on YouTube."

She suspected there were thousands of similar videos out there already, but this one mattered to them because it was Ivy.

Tanner made the baby smile again, talking to her in a funny voice, and Candy filmed it. She even cut away to Yogi, who'd come into the room to see why the humans were acting like such goofballs.

Afterward, Tanner said, "I think we should all hang out together tonight to celebrate. How about if Ivy and I stop by and see you at work?"

Her heart danced. "I'd love for you to do that."

"Okay, then we'll meet you there." He looked down at Ivy and said, "What do you think, princess? Do you want to visit Candy and Yogi's class?"

The baby rewarded him with a drool-speckled smile, confirming their plans for the night.

Tanner drove to the studio with Ivy buckled in her infant seat. This was the first time he'd taken her somewhere by himself. But he was so damned excited about her newfound smiling skill, he couldn't sit still. He needed to get out of the house.

Once they arrived, he placed her in a cloth carrier that fit across his body. She was facing his chest, so she wouldn't be able to see much, not unless he turned sideways to give her a better view, which he intended to do while they were observing the class. Knowing Ivy, though, she might sleep through the entire thing. She already seemed on the verge of dozing off.

He entered the studio. By now, he'd become familiar with doga, as Candy and Yogi often exercised together at home. But he was curious to see it in a classroom setting.

Candy greeted him as soon as he walked into the room. He'd gotten there early, giving himself time to get settled in. Her students had yet to arrive.

"Is Ivy asleep?" she asked him.

"Just about."

"She looks cute, snuggled against you like that."

"You look cute, too." He loved seeing her in her yoga

outfits. Those long shapely legs. That lithe body. He stole a quick kiss, giving her a peck on the lips.

Candy was a loyal friend, a hot lover and the best nanny Ivy could have. Wanting to touch her again, he gave her another kiss, only a little deeper this time. Nonetheless, he was careful to leave room for Ivy, cautious not to sandwich her too closely between them. The kid was already packed in the carrier like a sardine.

At 6:00 p.m., the students started filtering in. The people came in all ages, genders, shapes and sizes. The dogs were equally diverse: two teeny-weeny Chihuahuas, a regal-looking poodle wearing a rhinestone collar, a wiry terrier full of spit and vinegar, a French bulldog with a comical personality and a potbelly, and a properly behaved Great Dane nearly as big as a pony.

Candy introduced Tanner and Ivy to the class. She called him her friend and boss, explaining that she was his niece's nanny.

A few of the women fussed over him and the baby, but he didn't mind the attention. He was proud to show Ivy off, what little anyone could see of her.

He stood most of the time, even if a chair had been provided for him. Candy and Yogi took their places at the head of the class. As far as Tanner knew, this was an intermediate group, even if some of the pooches acted like beginners.

While everyone got settled, the French bulldog and the terrier barely stayed on their mats and had to be coached with treats. After a short while, they calmed down and drifted into the swing of it. The purpose was for owners and dogs to spend time together in a therapeutic environment, and it seemed to be working.

Candy was an exceptional teacher, with Yogi as her

clever canine sidekick. The lesson started with a basic seated position, where the students breathed, chanted and massaged the dogs. From there, they did doggy sun salutations, which involved lifting the dog's hind legs to the sky. Another was called a triangle pose, where the person was standing, stretching and leaning forward toward their furry partner.

The expressions on the dogs' faces were amusing, especially during the pose that allowed them to lie on their backs while their owners stroked their tummies.

The Frenchie, with his fawn-colored fur and big bat ears, was Tanner's favorite. He was such an animated dude, either lolling his tongue or grinning in content-ment.

The class ended on a sweet note, with the owners placing one of their hands on their heart and the other on their dog's heart. Tanner had Ivy nestled against his heart, so he was already part of the love.

He glanced over at Candy, and they exchanged a smile. He didn't doubt that if Ivy was awake, she would be smiling, too.

When Candy and Tanner got home, they fixed din-ner and gave Ivy a bottle. Then, a bit later, after they put the baby to bed, they spent the rest of the evening in each other's company.

Once they settled cozily in for the night, they re-moved their clothes, getting ready to bathe together in the master bathroom.

He turned on the water and adjusted the temperature, and she added eucalyptus body salts. It was her remedy for relaxation, something she often did before bed, and tonight she'd invited him to join her.

"It's been a fun day," he said.

"I enjoyed it, too. It was great having you and Ivy in class." She loved spending time with Tanner and the baby. In a perfect world, they would be her husband and her child. But she couldn't change the dynamics of her situation. She couldn't claim the man or the baby, even if she wanted to.

He climbed into the tub and made room for her. She sat in front of him and leaned back against his body. It was a tight fit, considering how tall Tanner was, but that only made it cozier, warmer and more romantic.

"I haven't taken a bath since I was kid," he said.

She smiled. She knew he meant that he was a shower guy, but she said, "You've just been dirty all these years?"

He poked her rib. "Ha-ha. Silly lady."

"So what do you think?" she asked.

"Of taking a bath? I wouldn't mind having a few toys to play with." He paused. "Oh, wait. I do have a toy, don't I?" He removed his arms from the sides of the tub and slipped them around her. "A soft pretty toy."

She sighed. "You can play with me anytime."

"Like my own personal beauty queen?" He teased her, brushing his thumbs across her nipples.

She sighed again, but he didn't linger. He lowered his hands to her stomach, his touch less sexual.

He asked, "Did you keep any of your tiaras?"

"I saved all of them. As much as I hated those pageants, I couldn't bear to throw away my prizes."

"You worked hard for them."

"Yes, I did." She dipped a washcloth in the water, then wrung it over her skin, making droplets fall from the fabric. "Maybe I should give them to Ivy. With her being a princess and all."

"You'd do that? You'd give them to her?"

"Why not? I love her as if she's…" She let her sentence trail, stopping short of saying the rest.

"Your own daughter?" He finished it for her.

She squeezed her eyes shut. "Yes."

"I love her that way, too. But she's not mine. She's Meagan's, and at some point my sister is going to have to reclaim her child."

Candy opened her eyes and stared at the wall in front of her. "At least you'll always be part of Ivy's life. You'll always be her uncle."

"And you'll always be her very first nanny."

"Better me than Mary Poppins?"

"Definitely better." He kissed the side of her face, nuzzling her hair.

They went silent, soaking in the tub, no more words between them. When the water lost its warmth, they got out, and she reached for a towel.

"Don't dry off," he said.

"Why not?"

"Because I want to be with you, just like we are, wet and sexy." He took her hand and led her to bed.

He turned down the quilt, and they crawled onto the sheet, making damp impressions with their bodies.

They kissed, soft and warm, and Candy could no longer deny what was happening. Not only did she love Ivy, she loved Tanner, too. She'd fallen for the man who was forbidden to her. The man she wasn't supposed to love.

With her heart in her throat, she pressed against him. How was she going to spend the next two years living with him and feeling the way she did?

She wasn't naive enough to think it would get better in time. She knew her struggle would only continue to progress.

So what should she do? Be honest and tell Tanner that she'd tripped and stumbled? That she'd become caged by their wild-and-free affair?

She hated to think of the trouble that was going to cause. She'd promised him that she wasn't going to get attached. She'd known there was a risk, a chance that this could happen, but she'd insisted to him that there wasn't anything to worry about.

Did that make her a liar? Or just a woman who couldn't help falling in love?

He lowered his head to her breasts and dashed his tongue across each nipple. He went back and forth, tasting the dampness that was already there.

She ran her fingers through his hair, wishing there was an easy solution. But there wasn't one. She had two options: tell him the truth or remain quiet, pretending that everything was okay.

As the foreplay got hotter, she clawed his skin, trailing her nails down his back. Tanner was doing delicious things to her, making her shake and shiver.

By the time he thrust into her, joining their hungry bodies as one, she made her decision.

To keep her feelings for him a secret.

Chapter Fifteen

Two weeks later, they took Ivy back to the prison to see her mother. Candy noticed that Meagan looked much better. At least her hair was clean and combed.

Unfortunately, she remained cautious around Ivy, not interacting with her daughter any more than she had before, even if she looked as if she wanted to. Clearly, she was still feeling inadequate, afraid of not being able to be a full-time mom to her little girl.

"Do you see how much she's changed?" Tanner asked his sister. "She does all kinds of cool stuff. She swipes at her toys, and sometimes she's able to grab them and put them in her mouth. She likes looking into people's faces, and she can support her head and neck without wobbling. She's even starting to do these mini push-ups. And man, can she smile. But she's been doing that for a while."

"Yes, I noticed how much she's changed," Meagan said, as Candy gave Ivy a bottle. "You guys are doing a wonderful job with her. She seems like a really happy baby."

"She is," he replied. "But she still needs you, sis."

"Given the circumstances, I think she needs you more than she needs me. So please don't pressure me about it. All I'm doing is considering what's best for my daughter."

He frowned, his frustration obvious. But Candy agreed that he shouldn't push, not while Meagan was still struggling to come to terms with her situation. Life was difficult enough without making it more complicated. Not that Candy hadn't done that. She battled each day, wishing that she hadn't fallen for Tanner.

Meagan sat forward in her chair, watching Candy feed Ivy. She was also studying her brother, as if she were analyzing his body language and the way he leaned toward Candy and the baby.

Then Meagan said, "Something is going on with you two. You seem even closer than you were before."

"Don't start in on that." Tanner frowned at her.

"I'll bet you're together now. Like a couple or something."

He blew out his breath. Clearly he didn't want to discuss his private life with his sister. "Even if we were, it would be none of your business."

"That pretty much means that you are. I knew you'd end up together."

He had a troubled expression. Candy was horribly uncomfortable, too, but mostly because of the secret she was keeping. To her, that made Meagan's observation worse.

When the baby stopped eating, Tanner picked her up. "I'm going outside to burp her."

"You can burp her in here," Meagan said.

"Yes, I could, but I need some fresh air." He shifted his attention to Candy, giving her an apologetic look. "I'll be on the patio if you need me."

She nodded and watched him leave.

Once he was gone, Meagan said, "Please don't get mad at me, too."

"I'm not mad. But my relationship with your brother isn't up for discussion."

"Why not? Because you're sharing his bed? Or because you're in love with him?"

Candy started, hoping the color hadn't drained from her face. "This isn't a conversation I want to have with you." Needing a diversion, she stood, trying to keep her feelings from showing. "I'm going to the vending machine to get something to drink. Do you want anything?"

"I'll take an orange soda."

Candy walked over to the machine and put in the money. Each can cost a dollar, and the first thing she did with hers was roll it across her forehead, using it like an ice pack.

She returned to Meagan, and they both sipped their drinks. At the table next to them, an older woman and her visitors were playing Scrabble. Candy wished that she was immersed in a board game, instead of gazing at Tanner's sister in emotionally draining silence.

Meagan softly said, "You are in love with him. Aren't you?"

Candy hadn't revealed her secret to anyone, not even

Dana. She'd been too stressed to do anything but keep it guiltily to herself. "You have no right to ask me that."

"Please, just tell me."

"I'm not discussing this with you."

"Well, I can tell that you are. And I can tell that you love my daughter, too." Meagan sighed. "I wish she was yours. Yours and Tanner's. It would make so much more sense for you to be her parents."

"You shouldn't keep saying things like that."

"But I'll never be half the mom you are to Ivy."

"Someday you're going to make a wonderful mother. You just need to work toward it. And please remember that I'm not Ivy's mom. I'm her nanny."

"The nanny who loves my brother."

"Stop saying that."

"Fine, but you know what I think? That he loves you, too, and he doesn't even know it. Some men can be clueless that way. He's never been in love before, so he doesn't recognize the signs. But I can tell."

Candy's heart lurched. "You don't know what you're talking about."

"Yes, I do. And if you love him you should tell him how you feel."

Candy didn't want to put herself in that position. It would kill her if Tanner rejected her. She couldn't take that kind of pain. It would be Vince all over again.

"I wish you and Tanner could get married and adopt Ivy. You guys would be such awesome parents."

"Oh, Meagan." Candy shook her head. "Please, stop trying to give your daughter away. And no matter what you seem to think, your brother isn't going to be the man I'm going to marry."

"But he'd be a good husband. Now that he has you and Ivy, he's the happiest I've ever seen him."

Candy still couldn't let herself fall into the trap his sister was trying to set. Tanner wouldn't be happy if he knew how Candy felt about him. "Just stop it, okay? Stop trying to push me into his arms."

"As far as I'm concerned, you're already there." Meagan took another sip of her soda, then motioned toward the door. "He's coming back in."

Sure enough, there was Tanner. He resumed his seat next to Candy and placed Ivy in her infant seat. The baby smiled at Meagan, and the young mother got tears in her eyes.

But just as quickly Meagan turned to her brother and said, "I want you and Candy to adopt my daughter."

He made a frustrated sound. "Give it a rest, Meagan. You know we can't do that."

"You most certainly can. You're both perfect for her and for each other. It's crazy that you can't see what's happening in front of your own face."

Candy's stomach went tight, the soda she'd drunk turning sour. She squeezed the can, bracing herself, sensing she was about to be thrown under the bus.

And then Meagan did it. She said to her brother, "Candy is in love with you."

He snapped back, "No, she isn't."

"Yes, she is. She wouldn't admit it to me, but I can tell. You don't have to take my word for it, though. When you leave here, when you're alone and looking into her eyes, you can ask her yourself."

Tanner barely spoke to Candy on the way home, let alone looked into her eyes and talked about love.

If Meagan was wrong, wouldn't Candy have defended herself? Wouldn't she have told him it was bull? That she didn't love him? But she hadn't rebuffed the claim.

At this point, he didn't know what to think. He parked his truck in the driveway, and Candy removed Ivy from her car seat. Silent, they entered the house.

She carried the baby into the nursery. His niece was being fussy, as if she sensed something was amiss, and he couldn't deal with that, either.

He plopped down on the couch and dragged a hand through his hair, scrubbing his nails across his scalp. He wanted to slam back out of the house and escape the panic that had come over him. But he stayed put, knowing that running away wasn't going to save him. He was going to have to face a discussion with Candy.

About twenty minutes later, she came into the living room and said, "I rocked Ivy to sleep, but I have no idea how long she'll stay down. It's been a strange day."

"For all of us." He finally looked into her eyes, the way his sister had told him to do. "Is it true? What Meagan said?"

She sat in a chair across from him, careful, it seemed, not to get too close. "Yes, it's true. I wish I could say that it isn't, but now that it's out in the open, I'm not going to sit here and lie to you."

"You told me that it wouldn't be an issue." He reminded her about what she'd said on the day she'd approached him about being together. "No commitment. No attachments. None of that stuff."

She released a choppy breath, her chest rising and falling. He could tell that she was nervous. He'd gotten used to her mannerisms. Everything about her was beautifully familiar, making this moment even more uncomfortable.

"I didn't do it on purpose," she said.

He didn't back down. He couldn't. He was just too damned flustered to speak calmly. "You should have known better. You with your wifely emotions."

Her temper flared. "You think I'm happy about this? That I wanted to put myself through this kind of agony? I tried to stop it from happening. I fought it, Tanner."

"Obviously not very hard."

"What do you want me to do? What am I supposed to say to make it better? I'm not asking for anything from you. I'm not expecting anything."

Nonetheless, he felt as if he was losing his mind, as if he actually had a wife and child. "I can't handle it."

"There's nothing for you to handle. I'll move into the guesthouse, and when you find a new nanny, I'll go back to Eric and Dana's."

"You're quitting?" He didn't want her to leave, yet knew it made no sense for her to stay. "Ivy will miss you."

"I'll miss her, too, but I can't cope with seeing you every day. Not like this."

"But you were going to stay here and not tell me that you loved me? How is that any different?"

"It just is."

"But how?" he asked again, needing an answer.

"Because I knew you'd punish me for feeling the way I do."

"I'm not trying to punish you." He was scared. Afraid of the panic and the pain. "I never wanted a relationship because I never wanted to experience anything even remotely similar to my parents' divorce."

"That isn't what's happening here. We're not married, and we're not going through a divorce. It's not the same thing."

"It feels the same. Now that you love me, everything is going wrong."

"Maybe what's wrong is your inability to love me back." She clutched the sides of the chair. "Do you want to hear something funny? Meagan thinks that maybe you love me already and don't even know it."

His fear went deeper. He didn't want to think about the possibility of being in love. He didn't want to be accused of having those types of feelings and certainly not by his sister.

Candy stood up. "Don't worry. I'm not foolish enough to believe that you love me. And I'm not going to put myself through the pain of hoping and praying that it will happen, like I did with Vince. I can't go through that again."

He flinched, hating that he'd been compared to her ex. "I'm not Vince."

"You're not destined to be my dream man, either."

He squinted, trying to not think about the nameless, faceless guy who'd been stirring his envy. "I'm not debating that point."

"I'm sorry that this is causing so much stress, but I'm not sorry for loving you. Maybe I should be, but somewhere deep inside, I don't think that love is something I should have to apologize for."

He didn't know if he agreed. He didn't know anything anymore, except that in spite of them not being married, he still felt as if he was on the verge of a divorce.

Tanner couldn't sleep. He'd gotten used to having Candy in bed with him. He hated rolling over and not having her there. He hated everything that had transpired today.

Was she awake, too? Tossing and turning in her room?

He didn't want Candy to move into the guesthouse. But worse yet, he didn't want her to go back to Dana and Eric's and leave him and Ivy behind.

He didn't see how he was going to be able to hire another nanny to replace her. How could he find someone as good and kind and loving as she was?

Loving.

The word made his stomach clench. What if his sister was right? What if he did love her?

Was it even possible to love someone without knowing it? He had nothing to base his feelings on, nothing to compare it to. Also, Meagan wasn't exactly the person whose opinion he should trust. She only wanted him and Candy to be a couple so they would make a lifelong commitment to Ivy. But he knew that adopting Ivy wasn't the answer. He wasn't convinced that Meagan really wanted to give up her child. He believed that she was acting on fear.

Tanner understood fear. But love? That wasn't within his realm of comprehension.

He glanced at the clock. It was five in the morning. He'd been up most of the night, batting his brain against the wall.

He wanted to talk to someone who could help him dissect his feelings, but other than Eric, he didn't know whom to confide in. And since Eric was already too close to the situation, with him being the husband of Candy's best friend, he thought better of it.

There was always Kade. Not that his brother was an

expert on love, but at least he was someone to talk to. Plus, they'd been through the same messed-up childhoods, with their parents' divorce affecting both of them in troubling ways. Tanner assumed that Kade had chosen a life on the road as a means to escape the past. But he couldn't be sure, as Kade had the tendency to keep his feelings to himself. Normally Tanner did, too. But this was different. He needed to let it out.

He dialed the number and waited while it rang. His brother came on the line and said, "Tanner? What's going on? Is everything all right with Meagan and Ivy?"

Obviously it hadn't been the best time to call. The early hour had set off a red flag. "The baby is fine, and our sister is a pain in the butt, as usual."

Kade laughed a little. "I hear ya about Meagan." He paused and then said, "I plan to visit her and Ivy when I can. But for now, my schedule is pretty heavy."

It always was, Tanner thought. But he couldn't fault Kade for staying away.

His brother asked, "So if this isn't about them, then what's up?"

"I'm just going through some personal stuff. With Candy," he added. He'd already told Kade the last time they'd talked that he'd hired his old high school girlfriend to be Ivy's nanny. "And now I'm trying to figure out if I might be in love with her."

"That's why you called? Dang, Tanner, how am I supposed to know if you love her?"

"You're not. I just needed to talk to someone about it."

Kade softened his tone. "All tight, so what's the problem? What's wrong with loving her?"

"Nothing, I guess. Except that I'm scared."

"Then you're going to have to work through that yourself. I can't help you get past the fear."

"I know. It's just that I've been alone for so much of my life, and now I have Candy. And Ivy, too. It's just so foreign from what I'm used to."

"I remember meeting Candy at Ella's funeral. She seemed like a sweet girl. And she seemed really enamored of you, even back then."

"She's still like that. Sweet, caring, giving. She admitted that she's in love with me."

"Then maybe you should figure out what's in your heart before it's too late."

"How do I do that?"

"Truthfully? I have no idea. But don't drag your feet, Tanner. If you wait too long, you might just end up losing the woman you love."

Chapter Sixteen

Tanner went into the kitchen to brew a pot of coffee, his brother's warning reverberating in his ears.

Could he live the rest of his life without Candy? Automatically, he shook his head, knowing the answer.

He couldn't. He absolutely couldn't.

He looked forward to every moment he spent with her. She was his best friend, his lover, the adoring nanny to his niece, and the woman he came home to at night. They watched movies together, they laughed, they talked, and more often than not, they analyzed the meaning of flowers. He ate the devil out of her home-cooked meals and made wild, wicked love to her.

Everything they did was immersed in beauty and joy.

How could he not love her? She was always there for him, his helpmate in every way. When he'd asked her to become Ivy's nanny, he'd referred to the primrose they'd seen at the park and the "I can't live without you" message that went with it.

A message that continued to hold true.

Now he realized why he'd felt as if he was going through a divorce during their argument yesterday. In a sense, he was already married to her—in his heart, without his even knowing it. Yet all along, he'd been worried and jealous about losing her to someone else.

Candy Sorensen. The girl from his youth. The woman who longed to be a wife and mother. He wasn't going to let her go, not this time. He needed to make it official, to become her dream guy and the father of her children.

But what if it was too late? What if she rejected him? What it he'd blown it already? He didn't like the sound of that, the feel of it, the possibility that he could lose her.

He prayed that it didn't happen.

He poured his coffee, then decided not to drink it. He was already wired enough. Besides, today was Candy's day off, leaving him with the responsibility of looking after Ivy.

When the baby's little voice played on the portable receiver he'd brought into the kitchen, he headed for the nursery to check on her. She didn't sound happy.

He noticed that her pajamas were soiled. There was even a bit of mess on the sheet.

While he was cleaning her up, she arched and kicked, whining her displeasure. He could tell that she was tired and wanted to go back to sleep.

"Okay," he told her. "But first I have to change your sheet."

He placed Ivy in her cradle while he got her crib

ready. Once the task was complete, he put her back to bed, his mind cluttered with thoughts of Candy.

After he left the nursery, he carried the soiled sheet and her pajamas into the laundry room and tossed the smelly diaper in the garbage outside. He washed his hands in the bathroom.

From there, he returned to the kitchen and came face-to-face with Candy, their gazes meeting across the room.

She was wrapped in her robe and getting ready to make breakfast. He noticed she was going to fix something for him, too, since she'd placed a package of ham on the counter, along with her veggie stuff.

Was that a good sign? God, he hoped so.

He tried to think of an appropriate greeting like "Hello" or "Did you sleep okay?" But he'd never been this tongue-tied before. It wasn't every day that a guy expressed what was in his heart.

She reacted to him just as awkwardly, removing a pan from the cabinet without speaking.

Should he talk to her now, before the meal got under way? Or wait until after they ate? He didn't know how to start the basic dialogue, let alone a marriage proposal. He wanted the sentences to flow, to make it as romantic as he could, but to keep it grounded in reality, too.

While he was debating his choices, a beeping sound emerged from the receiver that was still in the kitchen, signaling a dangerous alert on the baby monitor.

Candy spun around, and they dashed out of the room together. Tanner feared the worst. If Ivy wasn't breathing...

But his niece was fine. She hadn't even dozed off

yet. Her eyes were open, and she was scrunching up her face, getting ready to cry from the invasion.

He scooped her into his arms and shushed her, a flood of adrenaline still pulsing thought his veins.

Then finally he sat in the rocker with the baby and clutched her desperately close. Silent, he gazed at Candy. She, too, seemed as if she was trying to recover and remain calm.

As soon as Candy was able to relax and to stop her legs from wobbling, she checked the crib, trying to figure out why the alarm had malfunctioned.

She quickly located the problem. "The movement setting was on, but the sensor pad wasn't plugged in."

"Oh, cripes." Tanner made a terrible face. "That was my fault. I was so distracted this morning I must have jarred it loose while I was changing her sheet."

She heaved a laden breath. "Thank God it was a false alarm."

He shook his head. "I'm such an idiot. How could I have done that?"

"It's okay, Tanner."

"No, it isn't. I should have never been that careless." He stood up and put the baby back in her crib.

Minutes passed with both of them staring at Ivy.

Then he stepped away from his niece and said, "There's something I need to tell you and it can't wait any longer."

"About what?"

He gently replied, "About Meagan being right. I do love you, Candy."

Stunned, she merely stared at him, her throat catching. "You just had an awful scare. You're reacting out of fear. Saying things you don't mean."

"I do mean it, and I've been up all night, thinking about what love means and how it's been affecting me." He motioned for them to leave the room and let Ivy sleep. The baby was closing her eyes.

Candy followed him into the hallway, and they went into the living room. She sat on the sofa and tried to keep herself steady. "How can you love me in one day? Or decide overnight that it must be love?" That was too quick, too confusing.

"It hasn't been one day or one night, not technically. I just spent all kinds of time getting close to you, before Ivy was born and after she arrived. You've been there almost every second, helping me through it. You became my best friend, and then you became my lover. Isn't that what love is supposed to be?"

He made it sound so simple, so logical. But she couldn't accept what he was saying, not that easily. "What if you feel differently later?"

"I won't. If anything, I'll just fall deeper into you. Please, give me a chance."

He seemed so sincere, so honest, but she was still leery, her past rising up to haunt her. "The way I gave Vince a chance?"

"I'm not Vince. And when did he ever say that he loved you?"

"He didn't. But I gave my heart and soul to him, and in the end, he tore me apart. If I let down my guard, and you change your mind, I'll fall apart again."

"Now who's reacting out of fear?"

"I am." She clutched at her robe. "But it wasn't just Vince who hurt me. You hurt me when we were kids, too. You broke up with me. You left me. I can't take something like that again."

"But I won't leave you, not this time." He leaned against the fireplace mantel, with his thumbs hooked into his jeans pockets, looking like the teenager he'd once been. "I called my brother this morning because I needed to talk to someone, and he warned me that I could lose you if I messed this up. I can't live without you, Candy. I needed you from the start, and I need you now. Not just as my friend and lover, or as Ivy's nanny. But as my future wife."

His wife? Her heart pounded, torn between hope and fear. "You want to get married? You? The devout bachelor?"

His gaze searched hers. "After everything we've been through, is it so hard to picture us being married?"

Her pulse all but jittered. She couldn't begin to count the times she'd pictured them that way. "You do have husband qualities. I kept seeing them in you. But it still worries me that when push comes to shove, you might panic about being someone's husband."

"I don't want to be someone's husband. I want to be yours. And if I'm going to panic, it's going to be over losing you, not keeping you."

She wanted nothing more than to be his wife, but she hadn't been prepared for a marriage proposal, not from a man who might be making a decision he could regret later.

"I need some time alone to think about all of this." She pushed herself off the couch. "I'm going to go outside and get some fresh air."

"I'll be waiting, okay?"

Waiting for her to accept that he actually loved her?

To agree to be his future bride? To live a dream she'd never seen coming?

Candy went onto the front porch and sat on the steps. She could have gone into the backyard, where the garden was, but there were too many flowers out there. She didn't want their messages to cloud her mind. She was confused enough as it was.

While she was fighting the confusion, she glanced up and saw her mom's car pulling up to the front of the house. Oh, no. With everything else that had been going on, she forgot that she'd invited her mom to visit today.

That was the last person she wanted to see. But she couldn't do anything about it now.

Mom exited the car, carrying a sparkling gift bag decorated with a white bow—obviously the present she'd gotten for Ivy.

"I didn't remember that you were coming over," Candy said, feeling much too overwhelmed.

"Is that any way to greet a guest?" The older woman scowled at her. "And what are you doing sitting on the porch like a vagabond?"

Candy blurted out the truth. "Tanner says he loves me and wants to marry me."

"Oh, my." Mom dropped down beside her. "Do you want to tell me about it?"

She'd never confided in her mother, but today, she did. She went through every word, every emotion, everything that had transpired between her and Tanner.

Then her mom said, "I don't think it's odd that he loves you. It seems right up his alley to me. He agreed to help raise his sister's child. That already makes him a family man."

"Since when? The last opinion of him you expressed was that he had no business raising Ivy."

"I only said that because I was annoyed that you were hanging around with him again. I always believed that Tanner was the settle-down type. Now, Vince, he wasn't anything of the sort. You were always much more suited to Tanner."

Candy gaped at her. "I can't believe you just said that. You never even liked Tanner."

"I didn't like him because I was worried that someday you'd end up marrying him and having a passel of kids, and it would end your career. Tanner had a wild streak, but he still struck me as a boy who would want a wife. He withdrew after his sister died, but if she hadn't passed away and if his parents hadn't had such an ugly divorce, I think you two would have remained together and eventually gotten married."

Tears flooded Candy's eyes. "And now you think I should be with him?"

"It's what you want, isn't it? Besides, your modeling career has been over a long time."

"I hated modeling. And those stupid pageants."

"They weren't stupid to me. I loved seeing my daughter so poised and beautiful. And you were good at it. You worked hard to win."

"I did that for you."

"And it felt wonderful, seeing you succeed. I wanted you to be an independent woman with an uptown lifestyle. That's why I was happy when you got together with Vince. I knew that was the type of woman he wanted. A mistress, not a wife."

"Why did you want that me for, Mom?"

"Because that's the sort of life I'd envisioned for

myself. But I wasn't beautiful or glamorous. I didn't fit that mold. So I married a handsome man and had a gorgeous daughter instead."

Candy had to ask, "Did you love my father?"

Her mother frowned. "What kind of question is that?"

"An honest one. I mean, come on, why don't you ever talk about him?"

"Because it hurts. But if you must know the truth, I adored that man. I loved him beyond belief, and I was certain that someday he would become a famous actor. That's what he wanted, too. He devoted himself to his craft, trying to make it. But he died before he got the chance."

Candy couldn't have been more surprised. "My dad was an aspiring actor?"

"That's why he came to California to begin with. Then he met me and we got together and had you. But he never gave up on his dream."

"So after he died, you pinned your hopes on me?"

Her mom nodded. "I figured that somewhere inside you, you would have your daddy's ambition to be famous. So I put you in pageants, trying to bring out the competitor in you."

"Yet all I ever really wanted was to be a wife and mother."

"And now you have your chance."

"Yes, I do." Her eyes misted, her heart dancing on her sleeve. "To marry Tanner. To have his babies."

"Maybe one of your children will be in the arts," Mom said in her busybody voice. "Then I can guide its career."

Candy couldn't help but smile. "If one of them expresses an interest in Hollywood, I'll be sure to let you know. Speaking of children..." She gestured to the gift. "What did you get Ivy?"

"It's a dress." Mom removed it from the bag. The over-the-top garment was pink and puffy, decorated with ribbons and bows and lined with a ruffled petticoat. "As soon as I saw it, I knew I had to get it. It reminded me of the dress you wore when you were crowned Little Miss Princess."

Candy remembered that pageant well. It was her first win. Her first sash and tiara. She touched the fabric and said, "It's perfect for Ivy. Tanner calls her his princess."

"Really? Your dad used to call you that, too. He would have been proud seeing you win those pageants."

Candy got teary again. "Then I'll try to think of my beauty-queen days in a nicer way." She wiped her eyes. "Do you want to come in and meet Ivy?"

"I think I should do that another time. It would be better for you and Tanner to be alone right now. No doubt he's going crazy, waiting to see if you're going to accept his proposal."

They both stood up, and Candy put the dress back in the bag. "Thank you for coming by and for bringing Ivy's present. Your timing was perfect."

For once, her mother had made everything all right.

When the front door opened, Tanner jumped to attention, much too anxious to see Candy. As soon as she entered the house, he could tell that the news was good. He saw it in her eyes.

"I want to marry you," she said, falling into his arms.

He held her, burying his face in her hair. He had no idea why she was holding a fancy gift bag, but he didn't

care. All that mattered was that she was going to marry
him. He loved her, and she loved him.

She stepped back and told him about her mom and
how she'd forgotten that she was coming by. She showed
him the Little Miss Princess dress, too. He thought it
was incredibly cool for her mother to buy such a senti-
mental gift for Ivy. He was also blown away that she'd
encouraged Candy to be with him. That he was the man
of choice. The man for her daughter. He and Candy
were going to live happily-ever-after, with a few real-
istic bumps along the way.

"What are we going to do about Meagan?" he asked.

"What do you mean?"

"Now that we're a couple, she's going to press us
even harder about adopting Ivy."

She met his gaze. "Would you want to adopt Ivy?"

He nodded. He would take his niece in a heartbeat if
it was meant to be, but he didn't believe that it was. "I
would love to be her father and for you to be her mother.
But I don't think it's in Meagan's best interest."

"I agree. Your sister needs time to heal. She also
needs to gain the confidence to become Ivy's mother.
She shouldn't make any crucial decisions about Ivy's
fate while she's in prison."

"Then that's what we'll tell her. That we'll always
be here for her and Ivy. But no more talk of adoption,
not for now. Later, if Meagan still feels that way, then
we'll discuss it."

She asked, "Do you think that's going to be difficult for us? Wondering if Ivy is going to be our child
someday?"

"We won't let it be difficult. We'll love Ivy the same
whether she's our daughter or our niece."

Candy smiled. "I just graduated from being her nanny to her aunt."

"Yes, you did." He kissed her soft and slow, captivated by the feeling of being with her. "I want to dance with you."

He downloaded an old Backstreet Boys ballad from their youth and played it so she could hear the music, too.

She smiled. "This was one of my favorite songs."

"I know. I remember." He swept her into a rocking motion, and they danced and swayed, immersed in each other.

* * * * *

If you loved THE BACHELOR'S BABY DILEMMA,
don't miss the other books in the
FAMILY RENEWAL series from
Sheri WhiteFeather

LOST AND FOUND FATHER
LOST AND FOUND HUSBAND

And Kade Quinn's story...coming soon.

 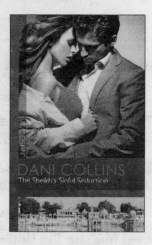
15_ST_9